MILES TO LOST DOG CREEK

as written by
RON SCHEER

Bonus story, "Origin of White Deer," originally published in the e-book *Adventures of Cash Laramie and Gideon Miles* Vol. II, October 2011.

With special thanks to Chuck Tyrell and Richard Prosch.

Cover art by Chuck Regan; design by dMix.

ISBN: 978-1-943035-10-6

www.beattoapulp.com

CONTENTS

MILES TO LOST DOG CREEK

– 1 –

Bellflower, Kansas. A huddle of weathered, wood storefronts and a scattering of barns and sheds. A rider came in off the dead flat prairie and stopped at the open door of the livery stable. "Anybody alive in there?" His voice echoed off the back wall.

"Yo." The answering shout from somewhere deep inside came after the echo died.

The rider got off his horse and stalked through the door, pulling aside a long dark duster to touch the grip of the Remington Army on his hip. He peered into the shadows and finally saw a figure step from a back stall. "I'm looking for someone," he said.

"Is that right?" the man said.

"Yeah. A weasely little fart. One wayward eye."

The liveryman paused, and leaned against the pitch-fork handle. His greasy dark hat cast a shadow over his face, but the long scar along his grizzled jaw seemed to gather light.

"He'd a been here two, maybe three days ago," the rider said. "Mighta been somebody with him."

The liveryman made his way back into the stall, dragging a stiff leg across the dirt floor. Then he went back to forking straw and horseshit into a wheelbarrow. "Lots of men ridin' together pass through here," he said. He shoved the pitchfork under another pile of straw and dung. The place stank of horse piss.

"We're having a conversation, asshole. Suppose you look at me," the rider said.

"Got work to do. You wanna palaver, go on over to O'Malley's. They talk a bunch there, in between the booze."

The rider stepped into the stall and planted a boot in the liveryman's backside. The force of the kick threw the man face first into the wall. He crumpled, and the rider was on top of him, straddling his body and shoving the long barrel of his Remington into the scar on the liveryman's jaw.

"Talk." The rider's voice was almost a whisper. A deadly whisper. "Everything. Tell it all. Every little bit." The six-shooter's barrel shifted to the liveryman's neck. "I said talk!"

The liveryman struggled to get his face out of a pile of wet straw, some of it in his mouth. He spat. "Mister. I don't know nothing … I got family. Wife. Kids. I don't wanna die."

"You don't talk, you got nothing." The rider chuckled. "You pitiful cripple, you got nothing. Maybe less than nothing. Now talk!"

"Tuesday, maybe it was Wednesday. Two riders. Yeah, two. Mighta been them you're lookin' for."

"The man with the cockeyed one. A half-breed?"

"Couldn't say. Nighttime, ya know. They was in a rush, too."

The rider put a knee in the liveryman's back and pushed. "Remember. Was he a breed?"

"Maybe. Yeah. Yeah. That's what he was, a half-breed. That's all I know. I swear."

The rider stood, holstering the Remington. He bent to pick up the five-tine pitchfork. A quick lunge and the tines pierced the liveryman's back, pinning him to the floor.

"Aaargh. He–e–elp."

"Woulda been a big help if you'da just paid attention." The rider put a foot against the liveryman's back and withdrew the pitchfork, only to thrust it in again. "Coulda helped."

A thin trail of blood leaked from the liveryman's mouth as he quivered, then went limp.

– 2 –

Gideon Miles stepped off the train at Overton, Nebraska, ten hours down the track from where he'd had a shot of whiskey with his friend and fellow U.S. Marshal Cash Laramie. They'd gone to a stockmen's emporium that afternoon so Miles could pick out a handsome sheepskin coat for his long winter journey, and then stopped by the social club for a drink before Miles left Cheyenne on a much overdue leave.

But why would a happily married man like Gideon Miles go to Overton, Nebraska, on vacation? Yes, Overton was a busy settlement that sat astride the Union Pacific tracks, but it was also still raw, with growth mostly from new settlers who came to lay claim to homesteads on the flatlands of the Platte River valley and go to work proving up on them. Two years ago, a colony of black farmers and tradesmen came to Overton, returning, so to speak, from Ontario, Canada. Miles' aunt Amelia had come with the colony, and he'd not seen her since he was twelve.

As soon as Miles got off the train, he went to see the marshal. Lawmen always paid courtesy calls on the local law, and Miles wanted the marshal to know he wasn't there on business. He had no arrest warrants in his pocket, and he was transporting no prisoners.

Marshal Lindquist turned out to be a tall, blue-eyed Swede about the same age as Miles. "Welcome to Overton, Marshal Miles" he said. He showed Miles a big, milk-toothed smile, and came out from behind his desk to shake hands. "What brings you to our fair city, then?"

"I hear there's a mild-mannered lady by the name of Amelia Wilson residing nearby, Marshal Lindquist. And I've come looking for her."

The beginnings of a frown creased Lindquist's brow. "Looking for Amelia, are you? Well …"

"She's my aunt, marshal. My momma's sister and my very own godmother." His aunt Amelia had lived with them right up until he was about twelve years old, and then she married a preacher man who dragged her off to Ontario in Canada. When he had heard that she'd returned, settling down in Overton, he'd finally made the trip to come see her.

"I know that woman, Marshal Miles. Godly, she is. That's the only word I've got to describe her."

"That's my aunt Amelia. Angel might even be closer."

"Well, her and Reverend Wilson, they live at the parsonage of the Holy Trinity Church over on Lincoln Street. Just cross the tracks and go east. Lincoln'll be the first big street you come to. Go south and you can't miss the church building and parsonage.

"My sincere thanks, Marshal. You've done me a big favor."

"Maybe you could buy me a drink over at the Station Hotel next time you're in town."

"Be glad to." This time it was Miles who thrust out his hand for Lindquist to shake.

Just as the two marshals shook hands, a voice came from a back room. "Lindy? That somebody come for me?"

Sounded to Miles like a boy. He leaned over to take a look through the open door into the cell area and saw a pair of hands gripping the bars—dark brown hands.

"Boy. Long as you're in my jail, you'll call me sir, you hear?" Lindquist gave Miles a wink.

"Who's your prisoner?"

Lindquist nodded at the cells. "We got ourselves a real, honest to goodness, cowboy outlaw in there. Come see."

Miles followed the marshal into the back room.

The prisoner was a boy with curly black hair and eyes wide in his brown face. He wore a wool shirt and vest, pants shoved into the tops of high-heeled leather boots, so he looked like a puncher. "You from Texas, boy?" Miles asked.

"None a' your damn business."

"See black cowboys up from Texas in summer and fall, but the leaves've already fallen. Why're you here? What's your name, anyway?"

"None a' your damn business."

"You said that, boy. But that don't make it so."

Lindquist puffed up. "Son, you look at that man good. That there's Gideon Miles. He's a U.S. Marshal who's probably put more bad men six feet under than you ever seen in your entire life. You be polite, else I'll paddle your bottom for you."

The kid looked at Miles sideways, his eyes wide, whites showing like a frightened colt's. "I'm Jimmy. That's my name. I ain't done nothing."

"Stealing a horse ain't 'nothing,'" Lindquist said.

"I only borrowed it. Everybody knows that."

"Borrowing without permission is stealing," said Lindquist. "Everybody knows that, too."

"The nag's my pa's horse. He knew I wanted to use it."

Miles listened for a sound of Dixie in the boy's voice, but there was none. Then it came to him. Canada. Of course. Jimmy's parents, or maybe his grandparents, must have traveled the Underground Railroad to freedom.

"Don't make much difference," Lindquist said. "If your pa wants you in jail to learn a lesson, in jail's where you're gonna stay."

As the two men walked back into the front office, Jimmy's eyes followed Miles. Haunted eyes, it seemed. Lost. Angry. And a little sad. Miles bowed his head and remembered the time when he'd owned a pair of such eyes. And not so long ago.

– 3 –

He called himself Way Gunn, but his true name was Waya, Cherokee for wolf. Him and Kit Kale had drifted up from Kansas. Kale called it "following our noses" whenever Gunn asked where they was going. Following their noses, said Kale, but it sounded like "looking

7

for trouble" to Gunn. Riding with a carouser like Kale could get a man powerful tired.

Like the time they'd fell in with the Boggs Hole boys to rob that Topeka train. That train was to be carrying the payroll of the Hutchison Salt Mine, but there was no strongbox on board. Nothing but a few passengers. The Boggs Hole gang just rode off, but Kale, he wouldn't leave without taking every red cent every one of the passengers had, all their watches, all their jewelry, anything and everything. He didn't even stop when he made that baby cry. He just took and took and took, 'cause that's how Kit Kale was—pure mean.

That handful of dollars didn't go far, not the way Kale spent them. Couldn't do without getting into card games. Couldn't do without whiskey either. And specially couldn't get along without whores. That's how Kale was.

Kale was good at cards, though. Gunn figured it was his wayward eye what did it. No one could tell where he was looking or what he was thinking, if he was thinking a thing. Anyway, he was damn good at bluffing, and he could cheat so no one could figure it out. He was lucky at lying and cheating, but he was a cold-blooded bastard and bastards have got to run outta luck some time.

Gunn could get real pissed at Kale. And he had to admit, Kale knew just how to get his goat, calling him a blanket Indian. "Your own ma was nothing but a squaw," he'd say. Then give out with that awful cackle of his.

"Kit Kale, you know it was my grandma who was Cherokee. Not ma." And he didn't tell Kale that his real name was Waya and that it meant wolf. Maybe someday he'd turn wolf on Kale's rat ass.

Kale'd shake his head. "Blanket Indian's worse'n a nigger," he'd say.

That kind of talk really got to Gunn. Time he went his own way and let Kit—whose real name was Christopher—Kale go his own way. To hear him tell it, he didn't need Gunn anyhow.

They crossed the Platte on a long wooden bridge that spanned all the shallow channels of that wide river. On the north bank, they come up on a hand-made signpost. One arrow pointed ahead to Plum Creek, the other pointed east to Overton. Kale, who as usual rode out front, paused and looked up at the slate-gray sky like he expected some kind of sign from the Almighty. Gunn just sat there, a little behind Kale, watching. Kale nodded, then reined his horse eastward, downriver. They climbed a low grade that took them over some railroad tracks and under some telegraph wires, and before long, a westbound locomotive roared by, throwing up dust and cinders.

"Hey, Kale. Where in Hell we going? You got some kinda surprise up your sleeve?"

Kale didn't answer.

They rode east, following the river and the rails past sod houses and shacks of nesters until they could see another settlement ahead. Just a cluster of buildings strung out on either side of the railway.

The streets were soft with winter mud, churned up by horses' hooves and wagon wheels. A few people hurried along the boardwalks—where there were any. Gunn followed Kit Kale past a school. They didn't stop. Then a lumberyard and a butcher shop. They rode on. A barber shop, a post office, and a newspaper. Kale and Gunn moved on down the muddy street. They passed a big dry goods store, and finally, across from the railway station house, they came to a two-story hotel. The sign on the train depot said OVERTON.

Before Gunn could move, Kale was off his horse, stretching, working the stiffness out of his back. Then he shook himself like some wet mongrel dog. He raised his own mud-caked boot up onto the mud-caked front steps of the hotel, and as he climbed the three steps up to the veranda, the spurs on his boot heels clanked.

Gunn remained in his saddle, taking a good look at the little hick town. His eyes went to the two women that came out of the hotel as Kale was about to go in. By the Almighty. They was black. Black as Java hens. Had it been white women, Kale'd a tipped his hat, but he didn't, and that was natural. That's the way things went.

Gunn forgot that his mouth was hanging open. He squinted in disbelief. Not only was those women black. Not only was they coming out of the only hotel in town. Not only that, but they was dressed like white women. They *acted* like white women, mincing outta that front door just pretty as you please. And no one said a word. Not a single solitary word. Gunn had to shake his head. Okay. So the Union won the war. But that was a long time ago. More'n fifteen years. So blacks was no longer slaves, thanks to Abe Lincoln, and he'd got his—a bullet in the back of the head. Maybe not slaves, but black is black, and nothing could change that.

— 4 —

Gideon Miles rented a horse from the livery just down the road from the marshal's office. He picked out a good-looking, black-pointed bay gelding and the rented saddle fit his posterior quite well.

As Lindquist had said, finding the parsonage was easy, and even though it was not quite finished, living there would pose no problem. Miles eyed the area. Nothing out of the ordinary caught his eye.

He got off the bay gingerly, hoping to track as little mud as he could into the house. He rapped on the door. A tall black man answered, and seeing Miles, a look of recognition slowly crossed his face, and then he threw the door wide open. "Brother Miles, brother Gideon Miles. I've looked forward to this day for, well, for more years than I can count right off the bat." He put his hand out.

Miles took the hand. "Reverend Wilson. Pleased. My aunt Amelia here?"

"Gid? Little Gid? My, how you've grown." Amelia Wilson nearly filled the doorway and Miles found himself hard pressed to keep from crushing his aunt to him in a huge bear hug. Instead, he gave her a peck on the cheek.

"Auntie. It's been a long time."

"Yes, too long. It's so good to have you here, Gid. So good. We're getting supper ready."

"I came all the way from Cheyenne, Wyoming, just to get some of your fabulous cooking, Auntie."

"Come in, then. Come in." Amelia turned to the Reverend. "Would you ask Mamie to dine with us, too, please? She's been working hard with those children and she needs to relax a bit."

"Right away," Reverend Wilson said, a cockeyed grin on his face. He left, headed for the barn-style building just behind the parsonage. The one with a white cross standing on the roof.

"That the church house?" Miles asked.

"And schoolhouse," Amelia said. "They're twelve families of us Negros here in Overton now. And you know as well as I know, that children uneducated are children who cannot reach their full potential."

Miles chuckled. Aunt Amelia hadn't changed a whit since he last saw her. She'd virtually beat the three Rs into his thick head, and look where he was today. U.S. Marshal, second only to Bass Reeves in criminals detained and cases solved.

Although unfinished, the parsonage was a comfortable place. One filled with an overstuffed sofa and easy chairs. And the kitchen table could seat a dozen people. What's more, the teacher named Mamie came early.

A tap came on the front door and Amelia answered it.

"Dear Amelia, I hope I'm not too early."

"Of course not. You can help in the kitchen, if you would."

"Gladly."

"Come. Come."

Miles and the Reverend sat in the easy chairs with a chess set on the table between them. The Reverend looked up when Amelia came in with Mamie in tow. "Hello there, Mamie." He waved a hand at Miles. "This here's Gideon Miles. Amelia's nephew and godson. He's here all the way from Cheyenne, Wyoming."

"Oh, my. Mister Miles. Pleased, I'm sure." She held out a hand. "I came from Chicago."

Miles stood, took the hand, and raised it to his lips. "Pleased," he said. The hand smelled good. And Mamie did not try to remove it. She left her hand in his, just a smidgeon too long.

He'd never written Amelia about Violet, the woman he called his wife in Cheyenne. She sang in a saloon, and might not be the type a reverend's wife would approve.

Still, as he was not yet dead, Mamie's attention stirred him. He felt the warmth arise, then she pulled her fingers from his hand.

Later, he found himself sitting next to her at dinner with several other congregation members gathered round the table.

"I'll say grace," the Reverend said, and bowed his head.

Miles listened as the Reverend said a long grace, giving thanks for the food and everything else imaginable. His words faded from Miles' consciousness as his attention focused on the lace trim at the schoolteacher's wrists. Then he realized the Reverend said his name, which brought him back from his divergent daydreams.

He felt his own body grow tense and wondered at being so easily unnerved when he'd remained cool in situations far more threatening—situations concerning life and death. Good thing Cash Laramie wasn't there to see his discomfort. Cash'd never let him hear the end of it.

"Amen," said the preacher.

"Amen," echoed the hungry people sitting around the table.

"Now," said Amelia, "we've got plenty of fried chicken, thanks to Brother Adams. And the Hickock family supplied us with collard greens to die for. We got hominy grits and turnips, and when you get through with that, we'll bring out the apple cobbler, fresh cream included."

Conversation lagged as they attacked the food. It was the best Miles had tasted in many years. He knew then and there that he'd been away from real southern food for too long.

Over apple cobbler, talk turned to the community.

"So," said Reverend Wilson, "let's take a look at what's happened to our community since we came. Of our thirteen families, all live and work on their home-stead land, 160 acres, with full intentions of proving up in three more years. But to strengthen our little gather-ing, we've invited more families to come and join us. Work to finish up the church building will commence in the spring. I assume you're all willing to help."

A chorus of 'yeses' rumbled from the now satiated diners.

"With the help of God the Almighty, we'll build a corner of Eden right here in the Platte River Valley. This, my brothers and sisters, is our Promise-Land."

"Right you are." The smiles on the black faces surrounding the table showed hope that few black faces showed these days.

In all the conversation and among all the introductions, Miles heard not a word about Jimmy. Not so many black people in town that no one wouldn't know a teenage boy with a Canadian accent. It had to be something they didn't want to talk about. But if anyone knew, it would be the schoolmarm.

"How are you finding our congregation, Marshal?"

"Just Miles, please."

"Not Gideon?"

"People call me Miles. I'm used to it."

"All right … Miles. Tell me. Is there someone special in your life?" She searched his eyes before he could answer. "There is someone, right?"

He nodded.

"Oh, well," she sighed, then changed the subject with a gracious smile. "What can I do for you?"

"I'm wondering if you know a boy named Jimmy? He's sittin' in jail for 'stealing' a horse?"

"Poor Jimmy," she said. "It's his father who's the trouble. He's disappointed in Jimmy, and I think it's his opinion that jail time will show Jimmy 'the error of his ways,' as they say."

Miles shrugged. "Didn't seem to me to be that much trouble."

"Yes, true," Mamie said. "What Jimmy really needs is a good influence. A good man to look up to." She gazed into Miles' eyes and put her hand on his arm as if to say he should be that influence. But all he could think of at that moment was the soft weight of her hand, and a warm, electrifying wave went right through him.

– 5 –

"You got a name, honey?"

The stranger didn't talk. He'd done no more than grunt since she first saw him downstairs at the bar. He'd stood alone, his back turned to some noisy cowboys—always seemed to be noisy cowboys around in this godforsaken town in north Kansas. But he'd nodded when she asked if he'd like some time upstairs.

"You gonna take off your coat and hat? Or just stand there?" She sidled up to him. He pushed her away.

She took another look at him. He was no country bumpkin. Not dumb. Not scared. He just stared at her. And it was a hard stare.

"I ain't got all day," she said.

He pushed her again. Hard. She fell back onto the bed.

She was a big girl, big all over. Some men liked that. Meat on yer bones, as they said. But she didn't go for rough stuff. She didn't have to. One good, long yell and the barman would charge through the door with a sawed-off 10-guage.

"Treat me nice," she said, "and I'll do you real nice."

"You're only a stinking whore and you'll do what I want." His lips barely opened when he talked. It almost sounded like a snake hissing.

Intimidation didn't work on her. She just thought of the 10-guage. "I'd say that depends on what you want." She'd known men like this. Under it all, they hated women. And even further down, they were afraid of women. Scared shitless. So when you got one of those crazies, you had to be careful.

"I'm looking for a man. Scum. You mighta seen him."

"What makes you think that?"

"He likes fat whores." He stepped to the bed and leaned over her.

"Lots a men do."

"The scum is short and he's scrawny. Got a funny eye. Makes you almost sick to look at him." His face was over hers and his breath stank of rotten teeth and chewing tobacco. She couldn't help but turn her face, seeking a breath of fresh air. His gloved left hand clenched over her jaw and wrenched her face around. She closed her eyes and a tremor ran though her body.

"Look at me, bitch."

She forced her eyes open.

"When I'm talking to you, you'll watch my face," he said, teeth clenched.

"I saw him. I did. Two days ago. He won at cards and wanted me, too."

"See another man? A breed?"

"No."

"Say where he was going from here?"

"No."

He glared at her. She wondered how a man could be so still.

"That all you wanted?" she said.

"You think I wanted a screw? With *you*?"

"You gotta pay, poke or no poke. My time ain't free."

He pulled a leather pouch from inside his coat and took a coin from it. "Here's your money," he said. With one hand, he caught her by the throat. "Choke on it," he rasped, and shoved the silver dollar into her mouth with his gloved thumb, which had forced its way between her teeth. He pushed the coin farther and farther down her throat. She gagged. Tears trickled from her eyes. She tried to shake her head, but couldn't. She had waited too long to scream for help. She tried to breath. She tried and tried. But she couldn't. No matter how hard she tried. She couldn't. Couldn't.

– **6** –

The Overton Hotel didn't have a room for Miles, or so he was told by a sallow, wheezing man at the front desk. If he could find someone willing to share a bed with him, though, well, he was welcome to try. That no one would share his bed with a black man went without saying.

Miles was in need of a place to sleep since he'd decided not to stay at Aunt Amelia's house, even though she and the Reverend insisted. Their home was full up with church family, and the unfinished parsonage and schoolhouse didn't offer adequate accommodations just yet. But mostly, he didn't want to betray his devotion to Violet, and if he'd stayed, Mamie being in such close proximity, she certainly was a temptation he felt he couldn't trust himself around.

So once more he was at the marshal's office, leather valise in hand. "Tell me Lindquist, there's no vacancy at the hotel. You know of anywhere in town that'd give me a place to sleep?"

"Aw, hell, Miles. Sleep here." The marshal's face wore a huge smile. "There's an empty cell and the bed ain't bad. I've slept on it myself."

He boarded at a house around the corner, he said, and Miles was welcome to sleep there with him. "But I've been told I snore bad and fart all night," he laughed. "You're better off here."

"Thank you," Miles said. "So, you still have your star prisoner?"

"Jimmy? He's still back there."

Lindquist dropped firewood into the pot-bellied stove, and settled back into his seat behind the desk. He dug a briar from the top draw. "Smoke?"

"Got my own," Miles said, and dug his own hooked pipe from his valise.

Lindquist offered a sack of Bull Durham, which Miles used to fill his pipe. He took one of the lucifers from the box on the desk and puffed the pipe alive. Smoking and talking just naturally went together, and the time edged on toward midnight. The marshal took a bottle from the bottom drawer. "Drink?"

Miles nodded, holding his thumb and forefinger apart about a half inch. "Little one."

"None for me," the marshal said as he poured a finger of rye whiskey into a pint jar for Miles. "Like to keep a clear head 'til I'm off duty, and that don't come 'til midnight. By then, all I wanna do is sleep. I guess drinking never was much of a thing for me."

After a time, the marshal stood, put on his gun belt and his coat before leaving to make the last round of the day. "A feller named Julius comes around in the morning," he said. "Old lawman, used to keep order in Missouri in the bad old days. To hear him tell it, he chased up the James gang until that Northfield raid. Let him know who you are, flash a badge at him if you have to. Maybe he won't shoot you." The marshal stepped out into the cold night.

Miles put more wood in the stove and carried the lamp into the back room. The door of one cell stood open. Inside, a worn patchwork quilt was thrown over the narrow bunk against the far wall. A shadowy form lay huddled on the bunk in the other cell.

The room was clean and didn't smell bad. He put his valise on the floor next to the head of the bunk where it would be within easy reach. He snapped the latch open. His gun lay inside, atop a change of clothes, loaded and ready should there be need for a firearm during the night. The valise also held a knife in a sheath that strapped to his arm under his sleeve, because he felt almost naked without it.

Miles blew out the lamp and took off his boots in the darkness. Then he lay on the bunk and used his sheepskin coat as a cover. The long day filtered through his memory—Aunt Amelia, the family and friends crowded around the dinner table, and Mamie with her soft touch and dark eyes.

"Mr. Miles? Sir?" A small voice came from the other cell.

He waited a moment. "Jimmy?"

"Do you think I'm bad?"

"Did you take that horse like the marshal said? Without your Pa's permission?"

Silence.

"Well, did ya?"

"Um, yeah."

"Then what am I supposed to think? You're not bad if you steal a man's horse?"

"I don't want you to think I'm bad." Jimmy's voice broke like he was forcing back the tears. A stark contrast to the belligerent young man he'd met earlier.

"Well, sometimes we get second chances," Miles offered.

"An' if we don't?"

"Time will tell."

"Yeah. I guess so." Then Jimmy didn't speak, and neither did Miles. Then came the sound of steady breathing. Jimmy slept, but Miles lay awake, thinking about what he was like at seventeen, how he rebelled and ran off. And how that could well have put him on the wrong side of the law.

The clock in the office chimed once, and chimed again. Loud voices came from outside, then the door was flung open.

"Inside, gentlemen." Lindquist's voice barked orders. A lamp flickered on as someone applied a Lucifer to its wick.

"Need help, marshal?" Miles pulled his gun from the valise.

He stepped through the doorway leading into the office. Lindquist held his own six-gun on two men who held their hands high. They jerked those hands a bit higher when they saw Miles with his gun drawn and hammer eared back.

"Some ruckus over at the saloon," Lindquist said. "Someone was cheating—at least some said he was— and this one here put a hole through one of his fellow card players."

"He pulled on me first." The man who spoke had one eye that looked in an entirely different direction than the other.

"The man was unarmed. What was he gonna do, shoot you with his finger?"

"He just got a bitty scratch," the other man said, a man too dark to be a white man.

"Yeah, good thing your friend can't shoot straight. You'd be in big trouble."

"Why you taking us both in?" the first one said. "My friend Way Gunn here didn't do nothin'."

"Oh, shut up." Lindquist pointed at the door to the cell area. "He's here on general principles. Call it prevention. Anyway, that man you shot will probably wanna press charges." The marshal gave the dark one a sharp shove. "Now move."

Miles was about to give up his cell, but Lindquist unlocked the other and put them in with Jimmy, who was now awake and watching wide-eyed.

Miles whispered, "Don't want to question your judgment, Marshal, but is it a good idea putting those two in with the boy?"

"Just 'til morning. I'll take Jimmy back to his folks tomorrow, whether his dad likes it or not. He's been here long enough."

Miles still didn't like the looks of it, and it showed on his face.

"Anyway, I wouldn't put you out in the street," Lindquist said, putting a hand on Miles' shoulder. "And long as you're in there, trouble won't happen."

Miles hoped the marshal was right.

– 7 –

A gray-haired man with a long, drooping mustache clomped into the jail with the first light of day. Miles met him with a drawn Colt SAA.

"Whoa up there, hoss. I'll be Julius. You'll a heard of me."

"I have. And I'll be Gideon Miles. U.S. Marshal out of Cheyenne."

"Shee-it." Most of the old Missouri lawman's teeth were gone from the left side of his mouth, and the ones hanging onto his gums were all tobacco-stained and crooked as an old picket fence. The fact that a well-dressed black U.S. Marshal faced him with a cocked Colt didn't faze him in the least.

"You after these poor excuses for men?" Miles waved a hand at the Lindquist's late night guests. "They sure ain't pretty."

"Dunno. Heard y'all had guests, so I come to have a look."

Miles moved out of the doorway. "Look all you want."

"You running this joint?"

"Was. I reckon you are now."

Julius peered at the sleeping rannies. Miles had kept them on the floor so Jimmy could have the bunk. "I seen all kinds. Some a lot worse'n these."

"How can you tell how bad they are?"

"Instinct. Got any coffee?"

"Damned if I know."

"How 'bout we take a look?"

Miles shoved the Colt in his waistband. "Lead the way, Mr. Julius."

"No 'mister.' Just Julius." Julius found ground coffee and there was a pot on the shelf, so he used water from the water keg to brew coffee on the pot-bellied stove. He poured some into a chipped cup for Miles. "Damn. You'd think a town'd have decent coffee cups." He poured a cup for himself, and set the pot back on the stove.

Miles sucked in a sip with plenty of air to cool it to drinking temperature. When they talked about coffee that could float horseshoes, they talked about coffee made by lawman Julius. Miles knew. He'd just tasted the truth.

After a few more sips, Miles excused himself and went over to the hotel. He looked at the newspapers that came in on the morning train while waiting to buy breakfast for Lindquist in return for the favor of giving him a place to sleep. The day had dawned overcast but mild. Frost melted on the windows, and ice hanging from eaves slowly dripped.

Marshal Lindquist found him in the hotel lobby on page four of yesterday's *Omaha Evening World.* There were stories of cowboy troubles, shootings, lynchings, a vendetta between the punchers of two rival ranches in Oklahoma, with four dead so far. Two Dakota cowboys had disagreed over how to dispose of a horse thief and shot each other dead in a gun duel. The horse thief had outlived them—but only for a while.

Miles and Lindquist had just started into stacks of flapjacks when a shopkeeper in a white apron hurried in looking for the marshal.

"They broke out," he said excitedly. "Those men in the jail. They took guns and beat up Julius real bad."

Lindquist was out of his chair, his fork clattering to the table.

They'd taken horses from in front of the dry goods store, the shopkeeper was saying as they ran back to the jail. And someone saw the three of them heading north out of town at full gallop.

Three of them? Miles and Lindquist looked at each other quizzically.

At the jail, Julius was laid out on the floor, several men bending over him, and the doctor on his way. They stepped aside for Lindquist to kneel beside him, and for a moment Miles saw the bloodied, ashen face of the man he'd just met that morning, but he was grinning as he clutched one arm. The door to the cell where the prisoners had been stood open.

"Hell, I been through worse," Julius kept saying. "No need for all the fuss."

All three of them? Miles thought. *Why'd Jimmy go with them?*

Outside, the weather began to change. Fluffy snowflakes drifted down and melted on the muddy street. Miles checked the sky. The clouds were darkening in the northwest.

Lindquist stood in the doorway opposite Miles. "They musta cracked Julius one on the skull, and his arm's broke. Maybe his ribs, too. Now, where's that goldam doc?"

"What did Julius tell you?"

"Them rannies fooled him. Put on an act. They threw Jimmy onto the cell floor and jerked down his pants like they was gonna sodomize him. When Julius went in to help the boy, they jumped him."

"Was Jimmy in on it?"

"Not sure," Lindquist said. He punched the doorframe with his fist and swore. "Made a fool of me, they did. Julius is a tough old buzzard, but if anything happens to that boy—" He didn't finish the sentence. He didn't have to.

– 8 –

After crossing the Platte, the rider went to Plum Creek. He'd stopped at the general store, and people were talking about a shooting over a card game the night before. They said it happened at a saloon in the next town.

"What'll it be?" the storekeeper said to the rider.

"Can a' peaches."

The storekeeper stretched for a can on a high shelf. "Hope one of them tinhorn gamblers took a bullet," he said. "Whole bunch oughta be run clean out of the state, I say, every last one of them."

"No, sir," said a nester with a young wife. "They said the shot man was some relative of the mayor's."

The wife stood at the back of the store, holding up several yards of chintz to the wan light that leaked in from the front windows. "Brother-in-law," she said, not taking her attention from the bolt of cloth. She shook her head. "The choir director at the Lutheran church. Can you believe that? What in the world would a man like that be doing at a gambling den?"

"Who shot him?" the shopkeeper asked. He put the can of peaches on the counter. "Two bits," he said to the rider.

The nester spoke up again. "Drifters, they said, and the two of them're locked up. Mebbe both shot that guy."

"Mayor's in-law shot bad?"

"Bad enough."

The rider put down four bits. "Plug a' tabacca, too," he said.

The storekeeper pulled a plug from the tobacco jar and put it on the counter next to the peaches. "Owe ya a half-dime," he said, reaching into a pocket of his apron. He handed the rider his change. "There ya go."

The rider turned to the nester. "Where'd you say that feller got shot?"

"Overton, it was." The nester pointed down river.

The rider gathered his peaches and tobacco and left. Outside, snowflakes drifted down from slate-gray clouds. Some fell on his rough hands as he put his purchases in his saddlebag. He sniffed, then mounted the horse, and, kicking him into a gallop, he rode out of town.

An hour down the river, he came to Overton. The marshal's office wasn't hard to find. He tied the horse to the hitching rail, mounted three steps, and barged inside. An old-timer sat behind the desk, his arm in a sling and a bandage around his head.

"What can I do for ya, mister?" he said.

"I've come to see your prisoners." The rider stalked into the backroom. The cells were empty. "Where'd they go to?"

The old man laughed. "They busted outta here this morning. Roughed me up and lit out."

"You the marshal?"

"No, he lit out after 'em, couple three hours ago."

"How'd they get away?"

"Made off with some saddle horses that was hitched over by the dry goods store. One of the nags belonged to the Jew what owns the place. He don't take ta gettin' robbed a'tall. I can tell ya that. Mad as a wet hen, he was."

"One of 'em have a funny eye?"

"The horses? Dunno."

"The shooter, asshole." The rider's hands came up like he wanted to choke Julius.

The old man cackled again. "Oh, I gotcha. Yessir, that he did. Couldn't tell where he was lookin'. Seemed like two directions at the same time. I had a—"

"How 'bout other'n? What about him?"

"I was about to say I had a niece like that. Roman Eye they called it. Like half of her was asleep and the other half wide awake. Woulda been a pretty little thing weren't for that eye. She finally married a man what runs a wagon shop over in Kearney. They say he—"

"The other one," the rider said. "The. Other. One. Did he have a big nose?"

The old man thought for a long time while he stroked his mustache. "Now I can't rightly tell ya. Never did get a good look at him."

"Think." The rider pulled his coat back from his holster. "Remember."

The old-timer's eyes went to the gun in the rider's holster. "No need for that, mister. I'm a-telling ya everthin' I know."

"Which way'd they leave town?"

"North. Headed fer the hills, I reckon."

The rider went into the back room again to look around. "How'd they get out of here?" he called.

Julius laughed. "Well, that there's a long and amusin' story to some."

"I ain't got time ta laugh." The rider pulled his gun without another word and shot Julius through the eye. Now he'd never say nothing to nobody.

– 9 –

At first, the lawmen found it easy to follow Gunn and Kale and Jimmy as the tracks of their horses stood out in the new fallen snow. But as the day darkened and the snow fell more heavily, their tracks threatened to disappear.

Lindquist figured he knew where they were going. Ahead, past where Jimmy worked roundup, lay the Lost Dog ranch, deep in the Sandhills. "Bet you he'll head there for cover," Lindquist said. "But why would those two bastards go along?"

Miles was there for one simple reason. He wanted to find Jimmy and get him back to his family. The boy didn't respect Lindquist, but a U.S. Marshal of his own color might make a difference. He also felt like he owed something to Mamie, the schoolmarm. Like it or not, she made him feel responsible for Jimmy. She wanted him to be the good influence Jimmy needed so badly.

When they got into the hills, Miles could see that Lindquist didn't know much about tracking in the snow. They stopped to study the ground. "How far ahead of us do you think they are?" Lindquist asked.

"An hour. Maybe less."

"Damn the luck anyway."

Lindquist was still beating himself up for letting his prisoners get away, and Jimmy with them.

Miles himself couldn't help wondering what had really happened. Yes, the prisoners might have hatched a plan to fool Julius by acting out a rape. And they might have got Jimmy to go along with it. That might be a long shot, but the thing was, he'd only talked to the boy a couple of times.

What kind of trouble lay ahead, the two lawmen had no way of knowing. But trouble there would be. They knew nothing about the men they were following. There was even a chance the boy was a hostage. And if those men were desperate, Jimmy could be in danger. Miles had strapped his knife on before leaving town. Now its weight against his arm felt reassuring.

As they followed after the three jail busters, Miles fully expected the tracks to separate, showing that the two hard cases had left Jimmy to fend for himself. Then he had another thought. Jimmy might be the one taking them somewhere. He knew the country. Maybe he knew somewhere to go. A place to hide out. A place to take shelter from the storm.

In the end, Lindquist was right. The tracks led them to Lost Dog ranch, and they got there in mid-afternoon.

The snow fell faster and thicker, and the early dusk was settling in.

"Hello, the house," Lindquist hollered.

Lamplight appeared in one of the front windows, even though it was not yet dark outside. A door opened, a double-barreled shotgun muzzle came out, followed by a rough-looking woman. Her voice held a hard edge. "Who are ye an' wadda you want?"

She kept the shotgun trained on Lindquist's gut.

"Lindquist, ma'am, marshal at Overton. And this here's Deputy U.S. Marshal Miles. We're on the trail of some men that escaped our jail, and it looked like they might have swung by here."

She peered at them through the falling snow, holding the shotgun firm in line. "I don't know that I can help you," she said. "But you can come in out of the cold and have a cup of coffee, if you've got a mind to."

"Thankee ma'am. We'll just do that." Lindquist swung down. Miles stayed put. "Deputy? Lady says the coffee's hot. Come on."

"All right," Miles said, and he too swung down.

A man came striding through the snow, head down. When he realized strangers stood in front of the ranch house, he stopped short. He looked from one lawman to the other, his eyes squinted and his lips pressed into a tight line.

"Rankin," the woman said, "these men are the law, from Overton. I invited them in for coffee. You come too."

Rankin didn't move, but his eyes raked the lawmen up and down.

"I'm Iris Godwin," she said. "My husband's dead, else he'd be greeting you instead of me." Light from the lamp in her hands put a sparkle in her eyes, and her long, dark hair was not in a bun like most women around, instead it fell loose around her pale face.

"I'm sorry to hear about your husband, ma'am," Lindquist said.

"We lost Gerald to gastric fever, last winter," she said. She pulled her lavender afghan shawl closer around her shoulders. "We come west from Illinois in '82. For a while, things went well, but now we just have to move on without him."

"Yes, ma'am," Lindquist said.

"Come in, please. Coffee's hot." Iris retreated into the house, but not before Gideon Miles witnessed a look that passed between her and Rankin.

"Gentlemen," Rankin said. "Coffee in the house, the missus says. I'll put your animals in the barn, get them out of the snow."

He ain't no westerner, Miles thought as he handed Rankin the reins to his horse. That look. Could be that Rankin was set to take Gerald Godwin's place at the dinner table, and elsewhere.

The lawmen scuffed the snow from their boots on the scraper setup on the porch, then entered through the door held open by Rankin.

"Come into the kitchen, please," Iris called. "It's warmer in here."

"Yes, ma'am," Lindquist said, and he and Miles made their way into the warmth of the kitchen.

"Please be seated."

33

"Thank you, ma'am." Lindquist took one of the four chairs and Miles took the one farthest from the stove. Iris brought ceramic cups and poured steaming coffee from a large coffee pot.

"Sugar?"

"No ma'am. Black is best in my book," Lindquist said.

Miles nodded. "Black, please."

She poured black coffee for Rankin without asking, but added a spoon of honey to her own. Both she and Rankin seated themselves at the table. "Now, gentlemen. What brings you to Lost Dog Creek ranch?" she said.

"Well, Missus Godwin, to tell you the truth, we tracked three jailbreakers here to your ranch. We was wondering if maybe you seen 'em."

Rankin went and got a bottle from the cupboard. "Almighty cold out there, gentlemen. May I add some warmth to your coffee?"

"We try not to partake while we're on duty, Mr. Rankin, but …"

Rankin held the bottle out and gave it a tap. "Prime whiskey, gentlemen."

"Well, just a drop or two," Lindquist said.

The foreman smiled for the first time and chuckled as he tipped the bottle to their cups.

"You sure about the tracks?" he said, as he poured a rather large dose of the whiskey for himself. "Some of the boys went into town for the mail. Coulda been them you was following."

"Did three men go to town for the mail?" Miles asked.

Rankin didn't answer Miles. Didn't even look at him, just kept his eyes on Lindquist. "Wasn't all mail. There were supplies to be picked up, too."

"Mind if we talk to those men?" Miles said. "Maybe they saw something."

Rankin's eyes didn't move. He knocked back his whiskey and wiped his mustache.

"Reckon it couldn't do any harm," he said and turned up the collar of his coat. "I'll go over to the bunkhouse and get one of them."

"Rankin," the woman called after him.

"Yes'm."

"Don't forget to put the gentlemen's horses in the barn like you said you would. Poor things will freeze standing out there in the cold."

"Yes'm." And he was gone.

"It's almost dark already," Iris said. "Snow's still coming down. Seems the weather's turning bad. If a wind comes up, you'll end up riding in a blizzard." She paused for a moment. "You are welcome to spend the night here, gentlemen. There's plenty of room."

Lindquist didn't want to give up the chase. "If there's a way to track them jailbreakers down, ma'am, that's what I gotta do. Can't have people just breaking out of my jail."

Miles directed his question to Iris. "Ma'am, do you know a boy named Jimmy? If he was to come this way, is there some place he'd know to hide out? Some place other people might not know of?"

She shook her head. "I have no idea. Will Rankin's the one who knows the men."

Rankin knocked at the back door and came in without waiting for an answer. "I brought Red Haines," he said, and stood aside so the young cowboy could get in the door. Soon as he saw Iris, Red doffed his hat, loosing a wild shock of red hair. The breeze that came in with him brought a whiff of tobacco and horse sweat, probably from the wool coat the cowboy wore.

"Good to meet you, Red," Lindquist said. "Rankin says Lost Dog Creek cowboys went into town today. That right?"

A flush broke across his freckled face. "Yes, sir, marshal. Me 'n Black Jack 'n Billy, we went there. Went for the mail and to get the stuff, turned around, and rode back home." The boy's drawl tasted of Texas.

"About what time did you get back here," Lindquist asked.

"A hour ago, give or take."

Miles had a question. "Did you see any riders along the trail?"

Red shook his head.

Rankin smiled for a second time. "Well, looks like you've been on a wild goose chase," he said.

Then Miles had another question. "Was there any mail for the missus?"

Red looked puzzled. "Beg pardon?"

"Any letters? Newspapers? Magazines here for the house?"

The cowboy shot a glance at Rankin.

"He wouldn't know," Rankin said. "I handle the mail. And no, there was nothing for the house."

The cowboy looked again at Miles like he was waiting for another question. There was none. "I'll be leaving, then, missus." He clapped on his hat as he turned and nearly ran out the door.

"Reckon you two'll be headin' back to town then. You can probably make it before the snow gets too bad." Rankin sounded eager for them to leave.

"I won't hear of it," Iris said. "We have plenty of room, and it'll be a lot easier if they ride back in the morning. There's a roast in the oven with potatoes and carrots. Marshal Lindquist, please stay."

Rankin glanced at Miles. "Ma'am, is that such a good idea?"

She glared at him. Her back stiffened and she thrust out her chin. "I'll thank you, Will Rankin, to let me decide who can be a guest in this house. They will *not* ride out on a night like this."

"Yes'm," he said and put on his hat. "You need help with anything, you just holler." He turned to the lawmen and nodded. "Marshal Lindquist. Marshal Miles. I'll bid you goodnight." He closed the door firmly as he left.

To Gideon Miles, it looked like Will Rankin would not be moving into the house any day soon.

After the sound of Rankin's footsteps faded, Iris said, "I was thinking about what you asked, you know, about somewhere that might be some kind of a hideout. Well, there's one place that some hands might think was a hideout. It's an old line camp, up north of here.

Before barbed wire fences came along, the man we bought the place from said he kept a pair of cowboys up there all winter, every year."

"Is the line shack still used?" Miles asked.

"I'm afraid I don't know, Marshal. But it could be that our hands use it at roundup time. Though, this time of the year there'd be no one around. Nobody's got any reason to go up there."

"Up there?"

"Up for north on the one hand, up for uphill on the other."

"How would we get there?" Lindquist asked.

"Just follow Lost Dog Creek north. You know, the creek you crossed coming to the ranch house. It took my husband and I about an hour to ride there, but it wasn't snowing and it wasn't dark."

"We'll chance it," Lindquist said.

"The trail shouldn't be hard to follow. It goes right alongside the creek."

"We appreciate your offer of hospitality, Missus Godwin, but we've gotta get after them owlhoots."

Lindquist and Miles shrugged into their coats, settled their hats on their heads, and stepped outside. Miles put a hand on Lindquist's arm and held him up for a moment while he glanced around. Nothing seemed unusual. They walked through the snow to the barn. The horses stood inside, still saddled, tied to the top rail of a large feeding pen. A lamp burned, lighting the area where a cowboy pitched prairie hay into a rack along the wall for several horses. In the quiet, the swish of each forkful of hay as it fell seemed to be the only sound.

Miles leaned toward Lindquist and spoke for his ears only. "Take a look at the horses. Any you've seen before?"

Lindquist didn't understand at first. "Wha—" then the words took on meaning. He looked at the horses that jostled each other for the hay. He squinted as his eyes went from animal to animal. Then they stopped for a long moment. He nodded, and he led his own horse outside. Miles followed, ground-tied his horse, and shoved the big barn door closed. He picked up the reins, mounted, and went to catch up with Lindquist.

"Well?" he said.

"The bay with the star on her forehead? That's Greenberger's horse."

"Greenberger?"

"The dry goods man. His horse was missing this morning."

Gideon Miles smiled, but the dark and the snow hid his expression. "So they were here," he said. "And they traded for fresh horses."

"That foreman Rankin lied through his teeth."

"So'd the red-headed cowboy."

"Son of a bitch."

"Exactly."

– 10 –

Red stepped out of the bunkhouse and walked a few steps into the falling snow to unbutton his pants and piss in the weeds. The last light of day lingered on the silent blanket of white covering the hillside. A breeze began to stir the naked branches of the cottonwoods overhead.

"Here she comes," he said. "Gonna be butt-bitin' blue norther." Red had bet the Nebraska cowpunchers that a norther was coming. Being Texican, he knew about such things.

An arm came out of nowhere and grabbed him around the throat, cutting off air before he could make a sound. "Who you talking to, cowboy?"

The voice was barely a whisper, and Red felt hot breath against the back of his neck. It had to be one of the boys who'd followed him outside, Grady or Billy.

"Quit foolin' with me," Red managed to rasp, and he tried to laugh.

The arm tightened with a jerk that snapped his head back, and the voice came again, low and clear. "I said, who you talkin' to?"

Red couldn't tell whose voice it was. Then he thought maybe it was one of the lawmen at the ranch house, but then, he'd seen them ride out. "Just talkin' to myself."

He'd done his best to stick to Rankin's story about going to town for the mail and stuff, but that nigger marshal didn't seem to believe him.

The blunt end of what felt like a pistol pressed into his ribs. "You're gonna do some talking to me now." The ragged whisper sounded nasty.

"Sure. Sure. Whatever you want."

"Was there a couple of riders through here today?"

Red didn't answer fast enough so the arm tightened up and choked him till he could hardly breathe. "Yeah," he managed to squeak.

"A couple of lawmen after them?"

Red wheezed. "Yeah. Yeah. Who're you?"

He felt the arm release him and was about to take a deep breath when a sharp blow bashed him in the back of his head and knocked him to his knees. A kick spun him onto his back.

A man bent over him. "Suffering Jesus, I do not have the patience for this. Look at me."

Red had trouble focusing. He could only make out a shadowy face, dim in the falling snow.

"Those lawmen still here?"

"No. They went back to town."

A gloved fist hit him hard in the face, jarring loose a tooth. "Don't lie to me."

"I ain't lyin'. I ain't. I seen 'em head out across the creek."

"Then you're stupid. I'd as soon kill you for that as for lying."

Red panicked. "You ... you ... you can follow their tracks out of here," he screeched. "I can show you, I can, I can, I truly can show you which way they went, I really can."

"Oh, you will, will ya?" The man leaned back and stood up, his revolver still ready, hammer still eared back. "Off your ass then, and show me."

Red struggled to his feet. He got his hat from where it'd fallen in the snow, and jammed it on his head.

"Button your pants, asshole," the man said.

"Oh, yeah."

Fingers trembling with cold and fear, he fumbled at the buttons. It took him forever, it seemed, to get them all done up. He looked up at the stranger just in time to realize the man's revolver pointed at him. He opened his mouth to scream, but a bright flash from the barrel cut it off.

– 11 –

The wind began in earnest. It cut across them from the northwest, a gust now and then pushing hard against them, the cold sharp on their faces. The snow still fell, and it was beginning to blow along the ground. The tracks they were following eventually disappeared, first faint in the near darkness, then covered over.

The way ahead glimmered faintly. With Lindquist in the lead, they kept along the creek, its course dimly visible in the falling snow because of the willows that grew along the stream.

Miles tried not to think about what could happen— not find the line camp cabin, horses giving out after the long, winter-day's ride, or getting lost in the endless, unmarked hills, or freezing to death.

He did think about what was in store for them when they got to the cabin. The two fugitives were armed with rifles from the marshal's office. Things might not go well, unless Miles and Lindquist could take the jailbreakers by surprise.

As far as they knew, the men were petty criminals. Miles had known hardened men who shot to kill, even enjoyed killing. But what he'd seen of these two said they weren't mean enough for that. If somebody got killed while Miles and Lindquist were capturing those petty criminals, it would be from their stupidity or a careless impulse. And there was always a chance of that.

Be that as it may, Miles was really concerned about Jimmy. The boy had no business running with the likes of the other two. That'd only bring deep trouble to him. Despite all the decent, god-fearing black folk in the world, there were black thieves, road agents, even killers. Chances were they'd not been born to a life of crime, but somehow, somewhere, they fell under the wrong influence.

Influence. Back to the same thing again. Influence. His job was clear. Enforce the law. And always, always, always stick to the letter of the law himself. Thing was, he wasn't sure just how his job was gonna help him keep a boy on the straight and narrow.

They rode two hours, nearly three, before there was a whiff of wood smoke on the wind. They'd found the cabin—though the widow'd been somewhat off in her calculations of the distance.

Further on, a glimmer of light came down toward the creek. Light from a window in a low bulk of shadow on the slope. The lawmen got off their horses and led them through the snow to the willows along the creek bottom.

The long ride in the cold left Miles stiff, and his feet felt numb in his boots. The wind picked up, sighing and moaning through the bare branches of the surrounding trees, and sending snow flying to sting their faces.

"I say we go in with guns blazing," Lindquist said. "Get it over with."

"What about the boy? We don't want him getting hurt."

"He's been taking his chances all along. He can stay out of it if he wants."

"And if he has a gun?"

"Dammit, Miles, I'm freezing my ass off out here. Do you have a better idea?"

"I say we wait till we've got some advantage. One of them's got to come out sooner or later. Take a piss, a shit, get firewood, check the horses, get water from the creek. We can jump him as soon as he's out the door. That'll even the odds. And if it's Jimmy, so much the better. With him out of the way, we can go in with your plan."

"That could take hours." Lindquist's teeth chattered in the cold.

"Not if we give them some encouragement." Miles broke a thick branch from a tree, then another. "Someone once said that cats got killed by their curiosity."

The lawmen walked toward the cabin, and the wind whipped the smell of wood smoke into their faces as they went. Lindquist took a position in the dark next to the door. Miles tossed a branch onto the roof. The wind caught it and sent it skittering across the top. It slithered off the far side.

Miles pressed his ear to the freezing wall, but heard nothing, not even the sound of voices.

He threw another branch. It hit the roof with a sharp thud. This time someone said something. Miles hurried to the door, positioning himself on the opposite side to Lindquist.

An excited voice came from just inside the door. "There's a goldam bobcat up there. I've heard them scratch around before. I'll bet you anything it's one. I'm goin' out to kill that critter. Make me a nice pelt with its winter hair, sure will." The door flew open, the sharp sound of a cartridge being jacked into a rifle chamber came, and a man stepped outside.

He had taken only one step into the snow before both lawmen were on top of him, knocking him down face first. He let out a terrified scream, and Miles leaped to his feet, gun drawn as another figure appeared in the doorway.

"Kale, you okay out there?"

"Hands up," Miles said. "You and your pal here are going back to jail."

The man dived away into the dimly lit interior and Miles jumped after him. As he turned, Miles slashed the barrel of his revolver hard across the man's face. He crashed backward over a chair and lay on the floor,

moaning. As far as Miles could see, the dark man had
no handgun.

"Jimmy? You here?" Miles called.

"Here, sir," Jimmy answered, his voice croaking.
He lay on the floor by the stove, clutching a blanket and
looking sleepy. He sat up, eyes blinking in the flicker-
ing firelight.

"Are you all right?"

"Yes, sir."

There was the sound of struggle outside and then
another scream—this time of pain. "Keep that up and
I'll break yer other arm," Lindquist hollered.

"On your feet," Miles said to the man on the floor.

Lindquist dragged the one they'd jumped inside.

"You watch 'em, Marshal. I'll get some ropes.

Lindquist held the owlhoots at gunpoint while
Miles went outside.

– 12 –

When morning came, it pushed a wan light through the
single, shuttered window in the cabin. Outside the wind
roared, and came whistling through cracks in the walls.
Fire crackled in the stove, but produced only a feeble
warmth in the biting cold that invaded the room.

Lindquist opened the door. Snow had packed up
against it as high as his knees. "Good Lord Almighty,"
he said. "At least the sun's shining."

True, the sky was clear, but the roaring wind filled
the landscape with blowing, drifting white.

If the wind would let up some, they could make it back to the ranch before nightfall. If it didn't, they'd spend another long, cold night in the cabin. In that case, Miles and Lindquist would be taking turns standing watch over the prisoners.

Kale quit complaining about the arm that he swore Lindquist broke, and started in on Miles. "Don't see why you don't tie up the nigger boy, too," he griped, glaring at Miles.

"Don't see any need to," Miles said. "I'm the one wearing the badge, and if you know what's good for you, you'll keep a civil tongue in your head."

"I'll happily cut that tongue clean outta your head if you don't shut up," Lindquist said to Kale while he paced the room with a cocked Colt.

Miles glanced over at the marshal. Be good if Cash Laramie was here instead of Lindquist. Cash bent rules once in a while, but he had a level head. Above all, he knew he could depend on Cash. With Lindquist, Miles wasn't so sure.

He went and sat with Jimmy for a while, trying to get to the bottom of what went on. Why had Jimmy ridden off with the two prisoners? Did he run simply because it was a chance to get away? Or did the owl-hoots promise him something if he'd throw in with them?

Jimmy didn't like being questioned, and he wasn't ready to answer. In fact, it seemed he didn't have a reason for what he'd done.

Kale watched and listened. Miles figured he didn't want Jimmy telling what actually happened. "Don't believe anything that lying little bastard tells you," Kale said. "It was all his idea."

That comment gave Jimmy his voice. "That's not true," he blurted out. "They made me do it. Said I'd be real sorry if I didn't."

"Bullshit," Kale said. And as he was about to say something else, Lindquist belted him across the face with the barrel of his Colt. Kale's hand went to a lip that puffed up, and a cut opened under his cheek where the Colt's front sight raked him.

Lindquist put the barrel of the Colt under Kale's chin and lifted it. "I. Said. Shut. Up."

Gunn said nothing. He'd said nothing for hours. He'd huddled as close to the stove as he was allowed, wrapped his arms around his knees, and sat like a statue.

When the firewood ran out, the lawmen decided to send him outside to get more from the small stack of wood piled against the back wall of the cabin, mostly pieces of limbs broken from the cottonwoods along the creek.

They let him go by himself, figuring he'd not run off with the wind blowing like it was. Running away would be a good way to die.

"How come you don't send the boy," Kale said. "Carryin' firewood's nigger work."

No one spoke.

"You like doin' nigger work?" Kale said to Gunn.

Gunn said nothing, but went to the door.

Kale's hands were tied, and he looked at Lindquist like he was expecting to get hit again.

"Go to hell," Lindquist said, and stared at the floor.

Miles simply watched. He took a seat on a bench pulled up by the stove. Jimmy sat beside him, silent and huddled in a smelly horse blanket.

Enough minutes had passed and Gunn hadn't come back with the wood. Miles listened. He heard the wind, but no footsteps, no clunk of wood, no scrape of soles on the step. More minutes passed. Gunn didn't return.

Lindquist stopped pacing. "You think that bastard tried to make a break for it?"

Without a word, Miles got up and went to the door. He stepped outside, and a gust of wind whipped around the corner of the cabin. Shading his eyes with his left hand, he saw where Gunn had stumbled when plowing through a snowdrift. He drew his Colt and he followed the tracks around to the back of the cabin. The snow dazzled a blinding white in the morning sunlight, but he saw Gunn lying face down. Snow, blown by the wind, already collecting in the folds of his clothes. Blood oozed from his head, matting in his long, dirty hair as it thickened in the sharp cold, glistening. Under his cheek, a crimson crust of blood-soaked snow. Beside Gunn, amongst in the scattered armload of firewood, lay a thick branch. It was long as a man's forearm, freshly broken, and spotted with red.

"Drop it."

Miles looked up.

A figure in a long dark coat, his hat pulled low over his eyes, held a rifle on Miles. Miles slowly bent to set his Colt carefully on the woodpile. One look at the man's face told him he'd never seen the hard case before.

"Hands up," the man said, motioning with the rifle. "Now let's go back inside. Slow and steady does it."

As Miles retraced his steps, the man followed. He bent over to pick up the Colt left on the woodpile before coming on around the cabin.

"Stop."

Miles stopped. As yet, he had no choice.

The man pushed the door open.

"Nobody inside make a move, or this one dies." He shoved the rifle barrel into the soft flesh below Miles's jaw.

Everyone in the room was startled. Kale more than anyone else. He fell back from the broken chair he sat on, and looked like he wanted to crawl down through the cracks of the floorboards.

The man quickly shifted the rifle, and dug the barrel sharply into Miles's ribs. "Get over there with them people. Boy," the man said to Jimmy, "pick up every rifle and every six-gun and bring 'em over here."

Jimmy sat in his blanket, his mouth hanging open.

The man shouted. "You hear me, boy. Do it. Now!"

Jimmy jumped up. He gathered the rifles, then lifted the six-shooter from Lindquist's hand, and brought them over. The man simply nodded at the corner behind him. Jimmy piled the weapons where he was told and went back to his blanket.

"Boots off," the man commanded. "Everybody."

As everybody worked to get their boots off, the man walked over to Kale, who sat on the floor, his hands still tied.

"You, boy," the man said. "Get his boots off, too."

Jimmy tussled with Kale's boots and finally got them off. Pale feet protruded from frayed pant cuffs, the socks more holes than thread.

"This won't take long, gentlemen," the man said. "Start counting this as your last hour."

Lindquist puffed up. "Who the hell are you?"

"Kale knows who I am. Ain't that right, Kale? Tell these men who I am."

Kale lay on his side, hands still tied behind him. "Don't, Webber," he pleaded. "Don't. Don't. Don't."

"Me and Kale go back a ways. Don't, don't, don't we, Kale?" Webber mocked.

"It wasn't my fault," Kale said.

Webber's rifle suddenly spat flame. Everyone dropped at the crash. Hit, Kale screamed and lurched to one side on the floor.

"Nothing's ever your fault, is it, Kale. I was six years in Lansing. Not your fault. Small pox took my little brother. Not your fault. So he never made it out alive. Not your fault."

The rifle crashed again.

Kale was flung onto his back, and blood began to soak through the sleeve of his coat.

"If you're gonna kill me, put a gun to my head and pull the trigger. Don't do it this way. Please." Tears coursed down Kale's cheeks.

Webber laughed. "What? And spoil the fun? Not a chance."

Miles was aware of Lindquist standing next to him, stock still and silent. Jimmy was behind them on the bench, his blanket wrapped around him.

"I want to see what you do when I shoot off your ears." Webber jacked another shell into the rifle's chamber. "After that, your knee caps. Then your nuts. One bullet for every year I spent in that hellhole." Holding the rifle in the crook of his left arm, the man pulled his revolver.

Kale groaned. The tears continued to flow. He hiccupped. "Don't. Don't. Don't. Do–n't."

Miles sensed a movement behind him, a fluttering under the blanket Jimmy had pulled over his shoulders.

"You thought you and your pal Gunn were so damn smart putting me and my brother away." Webber stood over Kale now. "Well, Gunn is in Hell, and you'll be too, once I'm through with you."

Miles shifted slightly to get Jimmy in his peripheral vision. A dull gleam. Then he could see a pistol barrel emerging from under Jimmy's blanket.

Webber threw a glance at Miles and the others. "I reckon these otherns'll be in Hell, too, when I'm done with all of 'em." He looked back at Kale. Jimmy stood, stepped around Miles, pointed the heavy pistol at Webber, and pulled the trigger. The pistol fired. Miles dove for the gunman. A flick of his forearm released the knife strapped inside his sleeve, sliding it down into his hand. He plunged the blade through the open coat, deep under Webber's rib cage and into his heart.

Lindquist sprang up and grabbed Webber's gun hand as he stiffened. He crumpled, and sank to the floor, a startled look on his face. Blood poured from the knife wound under his vest. The marshal turned to Miles and saw the knife in his hand. "Son of a bitch. You coulda let me know you had that."

Kale lay on his back, moaning. His trousers bore a dark splotch of urine, which spread in a puddle around him.

Miles bent over so Kale could see his face. "What's this all about?"

At first, Kale said nothing, his body shaking uncontrollably with gasping sobs. When he regained some composure, his voice was hardly above a whisper. "It was in Wichita. Everthin' went wrong. Ever'one but me and Gunn was caught. Him," Kale nodded at the dead gunman. "Him and his no-good brother was both shot up, so they couldn't get away. I heard the trial was quick. They was lucky they didn't get strung up."

"You believe any of that?" Lindquist said, looking at Miles.

Miles shrugged and nodded at the dead man. "True or not, you end up with the same thing."

Jimmy, who'd saved their necks, sat by the stove shivering.

– 13 –

"Where'd Jimmy get the pistol?" Lindquist asked.

"From your deputy, when they broke out."

"Where'd he keep it?"

"Underneath that horse blanket he always carried."

"He mighta shot one of us."

"The boy saved our lives."

"How? He missed. We'd all be dead if you hadn't knifed that bastard."

The wind started to let up at midday. They brought the horses from the corral and saddled up. Kale bled from flesh wounds but would live. He lay on the cabin floor, roughly bandaged, while Miles and Lindquist dragged Gunn's body in and laid him beside Webber.

They'd leave the two bodies there to freeze after the fire in the stove died. Scavengers wouldn't be able to get to them, and Rankin or someone from the ranch could come bury them when there was a spring thaw. It's the least they could do after accepting a payoff from the jailbreaking fugitives. Jimmy had explained how Rankin and Red had taken a payout from Kale to keep their mouths shut. This didn't come as a surprise to Miles who hadn't trusted the Lost Dog ranch foreman.

"I'm in trouble, ain't I?" Jimmy said to Miles as they closed up the cabin.

"Depends. The folks in Overton might be willing to give you a second chance."

"Could you put in a word for me?"

"What do you want me to tell them?"

"That I'm not bad."

"Not promising anything, son, but I'll see what I can do when I got back to the parsonage and talk to Mamie, Aunt Amelia and the Reverend."

Hands tied, Kale was helped onto his horse. Still carrying his rifle, Lindquist waited for a moment with Miles. He nodded his head at Jimmy as the boy walked to his horse and mounted. "Did you take that pistol from him?"

"I did. It's in my saddle bag."

"Good. I don't want him near it." The marshal's eyes were still on Jimmy, widening. "What the hell? He's taking off!"

As Miles turned to look, he saw Jimmy spurring his horse and galloping toward the willows that lined the frozen creek.

"I can sure as hell shoot that horse out from under him," Lindquist said, raising his rifle to his shoulder.

Miles pushed the barrel down.

"Let him go," he said, watching the boy race off across the snow-covered hillside. "If he doesn't freeze his ass off out here, maybe he'll learn a lesson."

†

About the Author

Ron Scheer (1941 – 2015), a respected member of the Western community, reviewed frontier fiction and other cultural interests at his influential blog, Buddies in the Saddle. He held degrees from UCLA and taught in the Writing Program at the University of Southern California. He authored *How the West Was Written*, volumes 1–3. Ron resided in the Coachella Valley near Palm Springs and is survived by his wife Lynda and their two children, Anne and Jeremy.

ORIGIN OF WHITE DEER

Edward A. Grainger
with Chuck Tyrell

– 1 –

He followed Crazy Ed Holland down the Outlaw Trail from Hole in the Wall in Wyoming through Unitah Flats and down the Colorado River to Moab and Mexican Hat. He caught the outlaw in the waterless waste called Painted Desert where they shot at each other from dunes and sandstone ledges.

His bullet hit Crazy Ed just beneath his collarbone and tumbled through his left lung to exit under his scapula, leaving a hole big enough for three fingers. Pink foam frothed front and back, and the wounded man would soon drown in his own blood.

The man gave Crazy Ed a drink from his two-quart canteen. His three-color paint stood patiently in the shade thrown by a tabletop knoll that started out red and went through pink and yellow and brown to sickly gray at its foot.

Crazy Ed gulped for air but his punctured lungs couldn't hold it. He swallowed hard and reached for a handful of the man's shirt. "Goldam you Cash Laramie," he said, struggling with the words. "Goldam you." He swallowed twice. Foam bubbled from his wounds. "Just who the Hell are you, anyway?"

Crazy Ed died before Cash Laramie could answer. *Who the Hell am I, anyway?*

After the Sun Dance celebrating his coming of age, his Arapaho father, Lightning Cloud, gave the boy a new name. "You are twelve years old," he said. "You know the forest, the trees, the birds, the small animals, the elk and the cougar, the wolf and bighorn, the bear and the antelope. Once in a lifetime, the creator sends a white deer, which is sacred above all animals in the forest. I name you White Deer. So simple a name, yet one that carries honor and pride. One blessed of the Creator. Wear this name proudly, my son. Remember. You are chosen, White Deer, you are chosen."

In the year following his coming of age ceremony, White Deer grew from a smooth-faced stripling into a tall youth who had to shave each day to keep his visage clean in the Arapaho manner.

He hunted that day. He passed up two deer, a doe and a young two-point buck. He knew the village needed the meat, but a good rack of antlers would yield tools for flaking flint and handles for knives, and mature hooves made the best glue. Silent as a shadow, he now tracked a big six-pointer.

White Deer watched the buck, which browsed near the edge of a small clearing. He selected an arrow from the quiver at his left hip, moving ever so slowly, as a quick movement would alert the buck instantly.

The deer raised its head, still chewing the rich grass it had cropped from the meadow. Its ears flapped, seeking any sound of danger.

White Deer nocked the arrow and slowly drew it back to his right ear. "Do not aim," he heard Lightning Cloud say. "Think. In your mind, see exactly how your arrow will fly. Both eyes open. See what the arrow will hit. Think what it will hit. Release the arrow, and let your heart guide it to the target."

Without conscious thought, the fingers of his right hand flexed to send the arrow on its way, but at the instant of release, a twig cracked and the buck bounded. White Deer's arrow thunked into the bole of an old oak. A flash of anger seared his chest, but he maintained an outward calm. Two warriors walked toward him, taking no precautions about the sounds they made.

White Deer's blue eyes were chips of ice. He stood spraddle-legged, an arrow nocked and held in place with the index finger of his left hand. The Dog Soldiers walked across the clearing as if they were strolling about Lightning Cloud's village.

"I see you Broken Nose. I see you Redtail," White Deer said. He didn't release the hold on his arrow.

Broken Nose spoke. "It was unfortunate that we warned the buck you hunted, but there is no time to butcher the kill. Lighting Cloud would talk with you in your mother's tipi. We bring his message."

Lightning Cloud was not a king, or even a warlord. He presided over the council of elders and proclaimed the decisions that were made. But to young warriors like White Deer, his wish was law.

"I hear you," White Deer said. He unstrung his bow and put it in a sheath to hang over his shoulder. Taking his small pack of provisions, he walked to the oak, pulled his arrow out, and placed it in the quiver at his side. He followed the Dog Soldiers along Fall Creek toward Lightning Cloud's small village.

Fall Creek. Years ago, the Cheyenne and the Arapaho fought a company of cavalry at Fall Creek, and the fight inadvertently swirled around a small group of three wagons. White Deer's birth parents died in that fight, along with two other couples and three teenagers. White Deer was the only survivor from the wagons. He remembered little about his parents, nothing of his father, and only a memory of softness of his mother, and her terrible scream. But the scream may have been from his dreams.

He was still upset when he reached the village. His jerk at the bearskin that covered the entrance to the tipi was too violent, and his stiff posture betrayed his anger. Still, he breathed deeply of the aroma of good tobacco and knew that his Arapaho father had important matters to discuss.

Lightning Cloud spoke. "Sit," he said.

White Deer took his time arranging himself cross-legged across from the chief. "I am here," he said.

Lightning Cloud's deeply lined face looked like a piece of carved granite. A hint of green in his eyes betrayed a fur trapper in his lineage somewhere. An old man nearing his fiftieth year, his once-proud mane of long dark hair was now shot with strands of gray. A single eagle feather drooped from a braid at his temple. He puffed at a ceremonial pipe, blew the smoke upward toward the Great Spirit, Creator of all things, then held the pipe out to White Deer, bluestone bowl on his left and stem to his right.

White Deer's eyes opened wide in surprise. Never had his Arapaho father offered the ceremonial pipe to him. He searched his father's face for a reason, but found none.

Lightning Cloud gestured with the pipe again.

Hesitant, White Deer reached for the sacred bluestone bowl. Holding it at arm's length and bringing the stem to his mouth, he drew in the acrid smoke, then blew it upward as Lightning Cloud had done.

He handed the pipe back to the chief, who puffed on it twice and gave it to White Deer again.

Another puff, and another. White Deer held the pipe for a long moment, then handed it back, his eyebrows raised in question.

Lightning Cloud stared at the bluestone bowl. When he spoke, he used the white man's tongue. Only he and his wife, Elina—White Deer's Arapaho mother—and Twisted Root, the medicine man, understood and spoke the white man's language. They had made certain that White Deer did not forget it.

"Your mother Elina lies sick," he said.

White Deer started, then scrambled to his feet. "I must go to her," he exclaimed.

"Sit!" It was a command.

His back to the chief, White Deer's shoulders stiffened.

Lightning Cloud's voice softened. "Please, my son. Sit. She will be there for you when we are finished."

Slowly, White Deer sat again.

Lightning Cloud puffed once more at the medicine pipe, as if to gain courage to speak to his son. "It has been too many moons, my son. While it is important to learn to care for yourself, it is also important to allow those who love you to see your face. I could command you. I wanted to command you, because of the pain your absence caused your mother ... and your father."

The chief raised his face to his son. Suddenly he seemed old and weary. The lines on his face deepened and the silver in his hair caught the firelight. "I was going to command you," he said again, "but your mother said no. She reminded me that you were more than a year past twelve. A man. Someone with the right to choose his paths for himself."

He stretched out his left leg. An old wound pained him. Without looking at White Deer, he said, "The time has come for our ways to part. The white man is pushing, always pushing. And now the Indian Agent says the Arapaho must move further north. Our southern brothers have no more *neneecee* buffalo, and hunters with long guns now kill in our land, too. Our small village will go north into the land called Canada. Word says the red coats do not tell us how to live."

"What of my mother?"

Sadness filled the chief's eyes. "She is not strong enough to go."

"Then take her to Fort Laramie. The bluecoats have doctors. Medicines."

Lightning Cloud shook his head. He slashed his hand in front of him as though killing an enemy. "No filthy unfeeling white man doctor who has no respect for our people will touch the mate of my heart. I will not have it. I have spoken."

White Deer bowed his head so his father could not see the tears that threatened to leak from his eyes. "Without my mother, this village is not my home," he said. He clenched his teeth. His jaw muscles rippled. He raised his cold blue eyes to meet the green ones of the man who had been his father, if only because he was the husband of Elina, the woman who saved White Deer, who nursed him through the days after his birth mother was gone, who was always there with a soft word, a loving touch, a tidbit to eat. Always there. But soon she would be gone ... Lightning Cloud had spoken.

The chief studied the young white man who was his son. He met the ice of White Deer's blue eyes with compassion. "My son," he said, "you fight so hard. Someday I believe you will come to see that the one you fight against most of all is yourself."

The medicine hut stood at the outer edge of Lightning Cloud's village, a domed structure of box alder woven with willow withes and covered with buffalo hides. White Deer bent low to enter. The scent of herbs tossed on the smoldering fire mixed with the scent of death.

"I would have come sooner," he said to Elina. "I didn't know."

The women watching over Elina smiled at White Deer, but gave him tiny shakes of their heads. Elina, his beloved Arapaho mother, was on her final journey. He lifted a hand to her dear face, now etched with pain. Even so, she gave him a tender smile. The women left the hut.

"A few days ago, or maybe more, I was fine," she said. "But now …"

White Deer's chest constricted so he had to fight for breath. His mother lay dying. "I'm so sorry, mother. I would do something, anything, to ease your pain."

Elina raised a feeble hand to his strong, square-jawed face. "You are here. It is enough. You are so strong, my son. But it is time. You must now make your way alone."

"I cannot," he said. His grief brought tears to his eyes. They streamed down his cheeks. Dripped from his chin. He didn't notice. Gently he lowered his forehead to touch his mother's breast. How frail. How bird-like. Her breath fluttered in and out.

"My son." Her voice was hardly a whisper. "My son. It is time to open the chest."

"Chest?"

"The wooden one that has been here since you came. Over there." She cast her jaundiced eyes toward the far side of the hut.

White Deer had often seen the locked steamer trunk, but had thought little of it. Now he found it unlocked.

"Look inside, my son."

He raised the lid. A flat tray fit into the top of the trunk. Only a few items: a locket, a roll of bills, some coins, a knife, a shawl, a Colt 3rd Model Dragoon revolver, a box of paper cartridges, some caps, a handful of conical lead balls. He touched each item in turn, and at last, picked up the locket.

"Our people got these from the site of the Fall River battle," Elina said.

Your mother was alive, though mortally wounded. She lived three days. She was so beautiful, with long dark hair, and strong face. So very beautiful, as you can see if you open the locket."

Elina coughed, wet and hacking. She shifted positions, seeking one more comfortable.

White Deer pried the locket open. Inside, a photo of a man standing beside a woman who held a small child. "My father? Mother? Who is the child?"

"You mother wore the locket. The images must be you and your mother and father," Elina said. "Is she not beautiful?"

"Why did they have to die?"

"Why do we all die? They were unfortunate, caught between Cheyenne and Arapaho on one side, bluecoat cavalry on the other. Your father killed by bullets from the white soldiers. Your mother was hit in the back by a Cheyenne arrow as she rushed to his side, Lightning Cloud said."

Elina coughed her wet hacking cough again. Blood flecked her lips. She wiped it away with a scrap of cloth. "Lightning Cloud carried her and you to the safety of our village. Away from Fall River, as you know."

White Deer examined his dead father. Bowler hat. Dark coat and trousers. A scarf tied at his neck. He smiled and looked happy. His dead mother was indeed beautiful. Strong cheekbones. Hair piled on her head. A slight smile. White Deer himself on his mothers lap. "Did she name me?"

"We do not know, my son. She never was strong enough to speak to us. She never spoke your name. You are White Deer, whatever other name the white man may give you," she said.

"I wonder," White Deer said. "Is there some reason why these things were kept secret?"

Elina's face reflected her pain. Pain of body and pain of soul. "My son, rearing a child, any child, is a great test of its parents. You, one so young yet one who saw things that even adults shrink from." She shifted her body to a new position, unable to find comfort. The words sapped her strength, but she continued. "Your father and I did not always agree on what was best for you. Lightning Cloud is good. He is a man of honor. He is a man of passion. And he loves you dearly, as if you were his own flesh and blood."

White Deer shook his head. "It cannot be so. Always he reprimands. Never am I good enough to please him."

"He is pleased. He also believes you can do much more, and if pushed, you can become a great man, a man of justice."

White Deer's disbelief showed plainly on his face.

Elina tried to smile, but her strength was almost gone. "My son," she whispered. "The little leather pouch. The one in the corner of the tray. Give it to me. Please."

He scooped the little pouch from the wooden tray and offered it tenderly to his mother.

It took almost more strength that she had to open the pouch. From it she took three arrowheads chipped from blackest obsidian. Each hung from a thick thong of buffalo leather. "Come close," she whispered.

White Deer bent close and his mother put one arrowhead over his head to hang by its thong from his neck. "The hearts of your Arapaho mother, your Arapaho father, and every member of our village live within the flawless obsidian of this arrowhead. Keep it always, that we may be with you. But remember this wisdom—the arrowhead is only as good as the shaft that bears it, the feathers that make it fly true, and the heart of the hunter who uses it. Use this arrowhead well, my son. The Creator be with you."

She went limp, and for a moment, White Deer panicked. "Little Dove," he called, summoning one of the women who attended his mother.

Elina opened her eyes. "Call my husband," she said. The woman hurried out. She closed her eyes as if very tired. "One more thing, my son. Beneath the tray you will find white man's clothes and a letter. Twisted Root says it is addressed to someone named Eh Van Jay Hick Kerry. No one has read the letter and I know not what message it bears. Members of our village say there is one called Hick Kerry in the white man's village of Cheyenne. When you are ready, seek this man. Find what your parents wanted of him."

The long conversation sapped the remainder of Elina's strength and she lapsed into unconsciousness, but she managed to revive and open her eyes when Lightning Cloud arrived. He knelt by her side, tears on his cheeks.

"Do not be sorrowful, my love, my mate. Soon the pain will be gone and I will await you in the world of spirits beyond the horizon." She struggled to hold up a hand.

"My son."

White Deer clasped her warm, dry husk of a hand in his.

Elina pulled at Lightning Cloud's and White Deer's hands until she brought them together. "You two," she said. "All that I love in this world. Be at peace with each other wherever you may be. Promise?"

"I promise," Lightning Cloud said.

"I promise," White Deer said.

"Good," Elina said, and closed her eyes for the last time.

– 2 –

The tipis came down. The hides were rolled up and placed at the bottom of travois. Lightning Cloud's people filled in the fire pits and scattered the rocks that lined them. A season after they left, no one would know a village had been there.

White Deer watched until the last travois-burdened horse was out of sight. He sighed. His people went to freedom in Canada. He elected to be alone, to work out his own fate, to become whoever and whatever he could become. To find out who he really was.

The winter came late, but when it hit, it struck with a vengeance. White Deer made a small shelter hardly bigger than a sweat lodge. Nearby a small stream chuckled under its sheath of ice. He weathered three storms that piled snow over the shelter, helping keep the warmth in. White Deer sometimes broke the ice on the stream and caught fish to supplement his pemmican. Still, his supplies would soon be gone, and he now had no mother to run home to, no village to seek shelter in, and no father to clap him on the shoulder when he returned with a deer, saying "Well done, son." He was alone.

The fact of his aloneness made the scars left by the Sun Dance of his puberty burn. He was alone. Yet not alone. He had the skills taught him by all of his uncles in Lightning Cloud's village, and he had the power and determination instilled during the Sun Dance. Today. Today he would hunt. Today he would feast on venison.

He prepared carefully, checking the condition of every dogwood arrow, inspecting his bow of hickory backed with buffalo sinew, and placing pemmican in a carry bag of tanned deer hide. He added the pouch containing the two leather thong-strung arrowheads that matched the one he wore around his neck. He needed his mother's help on this hunt. He donned the poncho-like cape his mother had made from the hide of the first buffalo he killed.

The white man's clothes he left in the old wooden chest, along with the Colt revolver and its powder and ball. A deer hunt was no place for a noise firearm. He paused a moment, then hung the locket on its gold chain around his neck. Perhaps his white mother would help with the hunt as well.

White Deer followed a game trail through stands of lodgepole pine and quaking aspen. The snow piled up against obstructions to depths of ten feet or more, and walking across any expanse with no trail was tempting fate, as the snow often hid sink holes that could break a hunter's leg. "Always walk the same paths as the animals," Lightning Cloud said. "The deer and the wapiti always take the easiest path. We should do the same."

At dusk, White Deer found the watering place. The stream curved sharply and the swiftly rushing waters kept it from freezing. Many deer, some antelope, and several wapiti used the watering hole, and left their hoof prints behind to tell their story.

"More than half a hunter's success can be found in his patience," Lightning Cloud taught him. White Deer set about making a blind from which to watch the watering hole. Behind it, he prepared a shelter, cunningly contrived so the heat of his fire flowed beneath his sleeping place and up out of the back of the shelter to be dispersed by the limbs and needles of a bristle-cone pine. He built a fire, stacked alternating sticks of oak and pine so they dropped into the fire as the stick ahead burned away, rolled into the poncho-like buffalo cape his mother Elina made, and slept until just before dawn. Something inside him said it was time to get into the blind as the animals would come to drink in the half-light of early morning.

He strung the hickory bow with care. He inspected five arrows and put them into his quiver. He checked the edge of his knife to make sure it was sharp. Then he went to the blind.

The blind was built so White Deer could take a step to his right and have an open shot at whatever drank at the stream. He put his sparse belongings in the blind and settled in to wait.

Two porcupines waddled down to the water when there was just enough light to see. They drank and disappeared into the underbrush. Nocturnal animals, they probably climbed one of the nearby ponderosas to spend the day.

A red fox came. Then a young doe, heavy with fawn.

The light increased.

A bull wapiti and two cows came. Too big for White Deer's needs. Then a young two-point mule deer that still had his antlers. The buck stopped short of the water and held his head high, sampling the air for a whiff of danger. His big ears switched back and forth, searching for sounds that did not belong.

So slowly that he hardly seemed to move, White Deer lifted his best dogwood arrow and laid it across his bow, nocked it, and held it in place with his index finger. Slowly, slowly, he stood.

The buck took another step forward and stretched its neck toward the rippling water. The moment his muzzle touched the stream, White Deer stepped from his blind and sent his arrow whizzing across the thirty-pace distance to plunge into the buck's side, just behind his shoulder. The arrow slid between the buck's ribs and through its lung tissue to lodge in its heart. The buck reacted with a high bound, then half a dozen leaps out into the meadow across the stream. Then it dropped, skidding across the frozen snow.

"*Hééteenew*," White Deer said. "I respect you. I am now going to share this feast with you, Man Above." He snatched up his belongings and ran to the dead buck.

He rolled the dead deer on its side and cut its jugular vein so it would bleed out. Hungry for meat, anything other than fish and pemmican, he cut the deer's belly open with his knife. He reached into the steaming intestines to find the liver. He pulled it out and cut it free. Liver. Hot, succulent liver. He cut off a thin slice and stuffed it into his mouth. The warmth flooded his body. The ironish taste made him smile. He cut off another slice. So intent was he on the food that he didn't hear the footsteps sneaking up behind him. All he registered was a blinding pain in the back of his head and blackness.

*   *   *

Cold. Cold. So very very cold. White Deer came to when the sun was well past the meridian. All he could feel was the terrible cold, and the throbbing pain in his head. He lay spread-eagled in the snow. He wore no buffalo cape. He wore no red flannel trade shirt. He wore no leather leggings. His hand went automatically to his throat. No obsidian arrowhead on its leather thong, or oblong locket on a golden chain. He struggled to his hands and knees. So cold.

He stared at the blood in the snow, all that remained of the little buck his arrow had felled. Arrow. He looked about, his near-freezing condition narrowing his field of vision. His hickory bow lay in the snow, broken in two, the fletched half of the arrow beside it. The buck was gone, along with his meager possessions. He took a deep breath and looked inside himself. He was White Deer. He was one of the people of this land. "Great Spirit," he said aloud. "My life is in your hands, but I would live to find those who desecrate my mothers. The ones who stole their talismans. I would find them and take my revenge."

A fire started deep in his heart. A fire of rage such as one so young as White Deer rarely found. A rage that helped him struggle to his feet to live. His eyes swept the scene, looking for clues. Boot tracks. The print of a rifle butt. Traces of the buck's carcass dragged between two lines of boot prints, across the little stream to where horses waited. Shod hoof prints showed they left at a walk. The robbers were in no hurry.

White Deer went to his blind. The robbers had found it. The rest of his arrows lay broken on the snow. The quiver was gone. They'd not found the possibles bag he'd left in the fork of a tree, above normal line of sight. Now he had some pemmican and his fire-making tools. He ate a mouthful of pemmican.

The robbers had not bothered to backtrack him to the little shelter where he'd spend the night. He took the broken arrow with the best point, because he had no knife. The arrow point with its sharp-edged flint must suffice. He built a small fire and warmed himself in the shelter. When he stopped shivering, he started planning.

Dressed only in breechclout and ankle-high moccasins, White Deer struck out for his base, the sweat lodge-sized hut he'd built to weather the winter storms. He ran, and the movement helped warm his body further. When he reached the hut, it was undisturbed. He plunged through the entrance. The chest stood against the wall. He opened the lid and removed the tray. He dug in the clothes and found a union suit, which he put on because he knew white men wore one under their shirts and trousers. The union suit was too big, but would do. A faded wool shirt hung loosely on his shoulders, and the old canvas pants were too long and too big around. He folded up the trouser legs and tied two bandanas together for a belt. There was even a floppy felt hat.

The clothing warmed him. He glanced at the wooden tray and noticed the old letter. He could not read the writing, but knew Elina had told him the truth.

Now is the time.

White Deer didn't touch the letter. He picked up the Colt revolver, checked its loads and caps, and laid it on the floppy hat, out of the way of any moisture. Cartridges and caps and bullets could stay in the chest. He decided to travel by day as he had no cape to ward off the cold, so he built a fire in the center of the hut, stacked wood so it would burn all night. Tomorrow he would start for Cheyenne. Tomorrow he would find Evan J. Hickey. Tomorrow.

He slept.

– 3 –

White Deer saw Cheyenne's smoke long before he saw the town. Raw as a two-year-old colt, Cheyenne consisted mostly of canvas tents and tarpaper shacks. Yet the makings of a city had already begun. The Union Pacific railroad ran east and west along the southern boundary. Corrals lined the rails on the southwest, waiting for the cattle driven up the Goodnight-Loving Trail from Texas. White Deer approached from the northeast. No one said anything to the boy in worn clothes, although some watched him drag the battered wooden trunk along the side of the street that fronted the railroad tracks.

Lightning Cloud said the buffalo liked this flat plain north of Crow Creek. Each season they came, he said, and the Arapaho killed them, not by the hundreds and thousands as the white hunters do with their long guns, but ten or twenty, one buffalo for each tipi in the village. But now, Cheyenne and the railroad and the white hunters meant no more herds of countless buffalo. White Deer wondered if Lightning Cloud's village found buffalo in Canada.

White Deer came upon a large barn with several corrals. It had a sign over the doors, but he could not read the letters. In the dim interior he could see a man mucking out the stalls. He decided to hide his chest behind an old wagon at the side of the barn. Lack of tracks said the wagon had not been moved recently. Its weathered sideboards were bleached a uniform gray and the iron wheel rims were red with rust. White Deer shoved the chest up against the barn behind the old wagon. He left most everything he had in the old chest, taking only the old letter, some of the bills, and three coins. The Colt revolver stayed there with its extra cartridges and bullets, but he took the arrowhead on its six-inch shaft.

He walked up the street along the railroad tracks until he came to an intersection where everyone seemed to be turning in or coming out. The new brick building on the corner lacked only a roof, and a boardwalk stretched up the block, inviting people to get up out of the dust of the street. White Deer turned onto the busy road and joined the throngs on the boardwalk. He'd never seen so many people and couldn't help wondering why they were in such a hurry.

A stagecoach thundered down the street, dust rising in a manure-fragrant cloud, and the driver shouting and hollering and cracking a long whip near the ears of the lead team. The rig flew by and White Deer caught a glimpse of the passengers grimly hanging on as the driver made his entrance. The teams and the stage plunged through the main intersection. "Hold up you motherless beasts," the driver yelled. "Stop when I yank on them leathers, you basties." He sawed on the long reins, bringing the teams around so the stagecoach came to a stop exactly in front of the train station. He said something to the passengers, but White Deer could not hear what.

He continued up the boardwalk. As he passed a frame building, he heard the tinkling of a piano, then the batwing doors flew open and a chunky man staggered out at a half run, windmilling his arms to catch his balance. He wasn't successful, and fell flat on his face in the dust of the road.

A big man with his hair parted in the middle and slicked down held the swinging doors open. "If I told you once, I told you a dozen times, Shorty. You're not welcome in the Bucket of Blood. Stay. Out."

Two women in low-cut dresses with lots of lace joined the big man.

The man called Shorty staggered to his feet. Squinting, he aimed a finger at the slick man. "Why, you, I just oughta …" Shorty's eyes rolled up and he crumpled, smashing his head against a hitching post as he went down. He lay sprawled in the dust, unconscious.

The women laughed. One of them looked at White Deer. He snatched his floppy hat from his head. "Hey cute boy," she said, simpering. "You comin' in? I'm getting tired of old duffers. Seems like everybody's over twenty-five. Coming?"

White Deer shook his head. He couldn't take his eyes off the twin bulges of her bosom.

"'S okay," she called. "Looks like you could use a haircut and a shave anyway." She disappeared into the Bucket of Blood.

White Deer watched. He wondered what people did in the Bucket of Blood. Shorty lay where he fell. Everyone in the street and on the boardwalk ignored him. White Deer decided to do the same. He started up the boardwalk again.

Halfway to the end of the block, he noticed a small building on the other side of the street. A star was painted on its only window with two words above it. A star meant a sheriff or at least a lawman. Lawmen knew what went on, who was who, and all.

He crossed the street, dodging men on horseback, farm wagons, and buggies, but he almost fell over a sleepy old dog. As he got closer, he could see a bald-headed man with mutton-chop sideburns sitting in a high-back chair leaned against the wall. He looked like he was asleep, his fingers clasped and his hands resting on an ample belly.

White Deer knocked.

The man jerked. "Huh? Wha?" The chair came down. He stood up. "Now you see, Sheriff …" His mouth snapped closed. He smiled, relief written on his face. "Thought for a minute you was Sheriff Adams." The man had a star on his vest. "How can I help you, son. I'm Rafe."

White Deer had not said a word aloud since Lightning Cloud's people went to Canada. "Um." His voice sounded rusty. "Um. I look for one man. One man name of Hickey."

Rafe looked at him for a long time. "Just who are you, boy? You got a name?"

"My father named me White Deer," he said. "I come here from beyond Fall Creek."

"Ain't never seen a blue-eyed Injun," Rafe said. "You a vagrant?"

White Deer frowned. "What is this … vay grunt? I am not one of those."

"Who'd you say you wanted to see?"

"Man's name, Evan Hickey. Evan J. Hickey."

"Judge Hickey? Why?"

"I have a letter for him." White Deer pulled the yellowed old letter from his trousers pocket, taking care not to tear the paper. He held it out to Rafe.

"Eighteen and sixty, it says. Boston." Rafe turned the letter over in his hand, but didn't open it. "Where'd you get this here letter?"

"My mother and my father were killed when the bluecoats and Arapaho and Cheyenne warriors fought at Fall Creek. This letter is almost the only thing I have from them."

Rafe studied White Deer's face. Finally he nodded. "I know Judge Hickey. His place ain't far from mine. I'll tell him you're looking for him when I go home in a couple of hours. That do?" He handed the letter back.

White Deer took a deep breath and nodded. He put the letter back in his pocket. "You have my thanks," he said.

"Got any money?"

"Money?" White Deer said, surprise in his voice.

"Yeah, money, moola, dinero. Whatever you want to call it."

"Yes."

"Show me."

White Deer dug the coins from his pocket and showed them to Rafe.

"Two-bit pieces. So you've got seventy-five cents. That's good."

"What about these?" White Deer showed Rafe a bill.

"Jayzus. A treasury bill. Fifty bucks. I'll be damned."

"But the paper and the coins, they are money, yes?"

"Ye-es, they are, but …"

"But?"

"Son, there's been a war, North against South, something you wouldn't know about. Now money's a bit different. So. Do you trust me?"

White Deer nodded. "You wear a star," he said.

"Son, don't you go trusting every man who wears a star. Some are crooked as a dog's hind leg." Rafe cackled at his own joke. White Deer didn't.

"Give me all your paper money," Rafe said.

White Deer hesitated. He wondered if he should tell Rafe about the other bills in the trunk.

"I'll take them over to Wells Fargo," Rafe said. "Get Elmer to change them for eagles or something." White Deer gave him all four bills.

"You wait right here. Fargo's just up the street and around the corner." Rafe clapped on a short-brimmed hat and left the sheriff's office at a brisk walk. White Deer could not help but notice how his belly jiggled. No Arapaho had such a belly. Maybe Rafe was like a grizzly, fat in the fall so the winter can be passed slipping in a cave in the high country. White Deer smiled. Rafe didn't look like a grizzly.

He studied the room. Square, with one window in front and one in back. One desk. Four wooden chairs lined the wall across from the desk. Some kind of yellow pot on the floor, made of brass. A squat metal box in one corner with a round dial and a lever handle. A rack with guns. White Deer stepped over to take a good look at the weapons. A long gun like the ones buffalo hunters used. A rifle with a yellow metal body, one that could shoot many times just by working the lever behind the trigger. Another gun with two large barrels.

He was still examining the guns when Rafe returned. "You sure as hell ain't no vagrant, kid," he said. "Four fifty-dollar treasury bills means you've got two hundred dollars. I got Elmer to break it up some. Here." Rafe sat down at the desk. He put a handful of coins on it. "Eight double eagles worth twenty bucks each. Three eagles worth ten each. Eight silver dollars and eight two-bit pieces. That's two hundred, kid. Can you handle that much money?"

White Deer wasn't sure, but he said, "Yes I can."

"Sure you don't want to leave some of it here? We've got that strong box." He pointed at the squat metal box. "Some of the people out there would slit your throat for a dime, much less two hundred dollars."

White Deer stood for a moment, thinking. Then he pushed all of the gold coins to Rafe's side of the desk. "I can get this when I want it?"

"Sure." Rafe put the money in the safe, then wrote on a slip of paper. "Here. This is a receipt. Bring it in anytime and I'll give you the coins."

"Thank you."

"Think nothing of it. Now. It'll be a while before I can get out to the Hickey place. You've got money, so here's what I think you should do." Rafe leaned toward White Deer like he was going to tell him a secret. "Goldaker's got a barber and bath joint over on Eddy."

"Eddy?"

Rafe stopped. "Sure. You just got here." He pointed out the window. "This street is Ransom. You just go down to the corner, turn left." Rafe gestured. "Keep on going west for four blocks. The fourth street over is Eddy. Turn south on Eddy and you'll see a sign with red, white, and blue stripes. That's Goldaker's."

White Deer gave a tentative nod. "Go to Gold Acre?"

"Yeah. Go get a shave and a haircut. Two bits. Then you won't look like no vagrant. Understand?"

"Yes, Rafe."

"Good. I'll go make my rounds. Oh, if you're hungry, go to the Bucket of Blood and order a nickel beer. They've got free lunch. You can eat all you want."

White Deer's ears pricked. Food. He'd not eaten for two days.

Rafe strapped a gun rig around his hips below the overhanging belly. See ya later," he said. "Just leave the door open."

Shave and haircut. White Deer reviewed Rafe's instructions in his mind. He left the sheriff's office to face the traffic on Ransom Street. He dodged a pale roan horse and its rider, slipped between two Murphy freight wagons, darted across in front of a rickety farm wagon with a bearded man and a stern-faced woman on the high seat, and leaped up on the boardwalk.

A roar from the Bucket of Blood stopped him. Rafe said it has free food. A nickel beer, he said. White Deer's stomach rumbled. Eat, then go to Eddy Street. White Deer pushed his way through the double swinging doors of the big saloon.

– 4 –

The batwings of the Bucket of Blood opened on bedlam. Miners, drummers, teamsters, conmen, railroaders, and a knot of soldiers in blue uniforms— perhaps a hundred men crowed the saloon, and they all seemed to be talking or laughing or shouting or banging their tables with cups or glasses or bottles. White Deer could hardly hear the piano, its notes a tiny tinkle in the cacophony.

No one paid any attention to White Deer when he entered. No one minded as he wormed his way to the bar. And no one remarked about his long hair and unshaven face. But the young dove who'd invited him in before saw him, and he saw her. When their eyes met, she raised her hand and waggled her fingers at him.

He bellied up to the bar when a small space opened between two drinkers. Three barmen served the crowd, hopping about like grasshoppers on hot skillets. The men looked everywhere but at White Deer. He raised a hand. No one noticed but the big burly man to his right.

"Hey Drafty," the man hollered. "Order here."

The barman called Drafty trotted over. "This kid? Order? Tell me, kid. Whatcha gonna pay with? Good intentions ain't enough. Show me some money."

White Deer plonked a quarter on the bar. "Got money," he said, his voice hard.

Drafty did a second take. "'K. Waddaya want?"

"Nickel beer."

Drafty drew the beer and slid it over to White Deer. He dragged the quarter to him and pushed back two dimes.

White Deer nodded his thanks and sipped at the beer. He wondered where the food was.

The burly man talked to the drinker next to him, and White Deer could just hear what he said over the bedlam.

"I tell you, and I'll say it straight. Ol' Evan Jay's got to be taught a lesson. A permanent one. Him sending my big brother up and all. I say we ride on over there tonight and give that uppity bastard what for."

White Deer turned his back to the bar as so many did, and his eyes just naturally sought out the young dove who'd first invited him in. She and a heavy one with the too-blond hair carried drinks from the bar to the tables. They deftly avoided grasping hands and laughed away lecherous comments. Then, as the heavy blond went by a table quite close to White Deer, a man dressed in well-worn range clothes took a handful of her generous bottom. She slapped his face like she'd done it a million times. "You can't afford any time with me, sonny, and handling the merchandise comes with a price. You pay, you get to tough and feel."

"Shee-it," the young puncher said. "All fucking high and mighty, ain'cha?" He turned as he spoke to the blond and his shirt front opened. White Deer went stone still. His eyes fastened on the obsidian arrowhead that hung on a thong from the cowboy's neck. One of those Elina had given him.

A scream half grizzly and half wild man tore from White Deer's throat. "You have stolen from me!" he cried. Drinkers backed away from White Deer, who strode toward the cowboy's table with his arm straight out, index finger pointing. "That is mine. *Mine*." He came to a stop, spraddle-legged, his finger nearly touching the arrowhead.

A flash of recognition showed on the cowpoke's face. Then arrogance. "Who the hell're you calling thief, Injun?" He swaggered to his feet like he was high and mighty, too good for a long-haired "Injun" boy.

"You got it right, Morlan. That un's plum Injun, you ask me."

White Deer turned his ice blue eyes on the speaker. He had White Deer's red flannel shirt on. "You," White Deer said, "you wear the shirt that was on my back."

Morlan cackled. "Hey Slim. Looks like he's calling you thief, too. What say we teach him a lesson or two in manners, how a Injun oughta speak to a white man."

Slim stood, chest puffed out, hands clenched into fists. He stepped over beside Morlan.

"Two of us're gonna kick the shit out of you, Injun boy. Thief my ass."

White Deer didn't wait for an invitation. He'd grown up in Lightning Cloud's village. Everything a boy did was meant to make him a warrior. Hardly a day went by without a fight, real or in contest. When a warrior fights, there is no such thing as fair play. Only winning. He leaped at the one called Morlan, slipping his arm around the cowboy's throat and throwing him in a classic flying mare. Morlan landed flat on his back, cracking his head on the hard floor of the Bucket of Blood. White Deer dropped on Morlan's belly with both knees. Morlan curled up and retched. Beer foamed from his mouth.

Casually taking the arrowhead from around Morlan's neck, White Deer stood to face Slim. "That's my shirt," he said, his voice cold as the ice in his eyes.

The Bucket of Blood went quiet as a church. All eyes were on the stripling Morlan and Slim called Injun.

Slim's eyes were wide with fright. He called for his tablemates. "Rush. Toad. Come on. We can get him. He's gotta pay for hurting Morlan."

Morlan retched. Bile came, flecked with blood.

The others joined Slim, but didn't look anxious to take on White Deer.

"Come on. We gotta surround him," Slim said, waving for Rush and Toad to go around in back of White Deer. They sidled sideways.

White Deer made no move. He looked at Slim, but his eyes were not focused. He concentrated on his peripheral vision. He stepped back and to the right, putting the table at his right hip. No one could attack him from there.

"You snuck up on me. I killed a deer and you took it. You took my buffalo cape. You took the arrowheads my mother made to keep me safe. You are not people. You are dogs."

Movement showed in the corner of White Deer's eye as Toad attacked. He stepped back, grabbed Toad behind the neck and used the cowboy's momentum to smash his head into the edge of the table.

"Ooooh," said the drinkers in the Bucket of Blood.

Toad's scalp split and blood splattered across the tabletop. He dropped face down on the floor and blood leaked from his head. He didn't move. White Deer ignored him. He faced Slim and Toad.

"Shee-it," a man said. "Four against one and that kid's beating the shit out of them cowpokes. My money's on the Injun, two to one."

"I'll take that. Ten dollars on the cowboys."

Bucket of Blood patrons formed a ring around White Deer and the cowboys. They shouted encouragement to the fighters and made bets. White Deer shut the noise out.

Slim and Rush stood separated by three or four steps. They put their fists up like pugilists. "Fucking Englishmen," someone said.

"Injun'll eat'm alive," another shouted.

White Deer didn't hear. He only saw Slim and Rush.

Drafty hollered from behind the bar. "You all pay for anything you break."

A man in a three-piece suit and bowler hat called out. "The Indian's half is on me."

Rush shuffled forward, his shoulders hunched to protect his neck. He jabbed with his left, nowhere near White Deer, who stood still with his right hand in his back pocket.

The would-be pugilist shuffled closer. A step away, he threw a roundhouse right that White Deer blocked with his left forearm. His right came from the rear pocket with a six-inch segment of dogwood arrow clenched in it. He plunged the arrow's head into the muscle of Rush's left shoulder, burying it past the barbs.

Rush shrieked and fell to his knees. He clutched at the arrow in his shoulder.

Slim, now desperate, lunged at White Deer, his arms stretched like he was going for a bear hug. White Deer took the half-full whiskey bottle on the table by its neck and smashed it into the side of Slim's head. The cowboy in the red shirt slumped to the floor.

Morlan retched bloody bile. Rush whimpered. Slim and Toad lay silent.

"I think that will be enough." The speaker stood slightly taller than White Deer, but he was heavier. Strands of gray showed in dark hair and his features were weathered and bronzed.

White Deer turned to face him.

The man held his hands up, palms out. "I have no quarrel with you, young man," he said.

"These are thiefs," White Deer said, waving a hand at the four cowboys. He pulled the arrowhead and thong from his pocket and slipped the thong over his own head. "My mother, Elina, made this for me. Now she is dead." He pointed at Slim. "That one wears my shirt, and someone has my buffalo cape. Two more arrowheads like this—" He tugged at the one around his neck. "—and a gold locket, too."

White Deer noticed Rafe standing slightly behind the man. "Rafe. These are thiefs. Take them. Make them give back what is mine."

Rafe looked at the man. "Whaddaya say, judge?"

The man smiled. "I'd say lock them up, deputy."

Slim groaned and sat up. His hand went to his head, exploring for damage. It came away tinged with red. "Sumbitch clobbered me with a bottle. Ain't fair. Damn Injun."

"Young man," the judge said.

Slim squinted. "Me?"

"Yes, you. May I ask where you obtained that bright red shirt?"

"Shirt? Oh. Yeah. Shirt. Um. Hanging on a tree limb? Maybe?"

White Deer's hard voice interrupted. "You lie," he said.

Slim held up his hands to ward off the blow he thought was coming.

"Deputy. Off to jail with them. Find out where the rest of this young man's possessions are and get them returned to him."

"Will do, judge."

The man faced White Deer. "Now. I understand you want to see me."

White Deer stared.

The man with the bowler put an eagle on the bar. "Not much damage," he said. "This should cover the broke bottle." He stepped over by the judge. "You carry yourself well, young man. And you know right from wrong. My name is Gillicuddy, and I own the livery. If you want to work, come see me."

"Yes … sir." White Deer nodded his thanks, but his attention was on the man people called judge.

"Come with me," the man said.

"I do not know you," White Deer said.

"Of course. I am Evan Hickey."

"Hickey?"

"That is correct. The deputy said you wished to see me."

White Deer tugged the old letter from his trouser pocket. "My dead father wrote this, I think," he said, giving the letter to the judge.

"Do you know the contents?"

"No … sir. I don't read white man writing."

Judge Hickey took the letter. "Hmm. Yes. It is addressed to me, but at my Boston address. Goodness." He opened the letter and extracted a single sheet. He read. "My God," he said in a quiet voice. "My dear God."

After reading the letter, Judge Hickey stared out the window of the Bucket of Blood for a long moment. "John said he was going west," he said. "He and Emily lost almost everything in the panic of '47." He looked up, seemed to see White Deer for the first time. He smiled, but his face seemed sad. "So John and Emily are gone these many years, then?"

"My father and mother were killed in the fighting between bluecoat soldiers and Arapaho and Cheyenne warriors at Fall Creek," White Deer said. "Lightning Cloud and Elina made me their son."

"Well. Come along. A shave and a haircut, then some good food. That will make a new man of you."

"Free food here," White Deer said. "Rafe say to buy nickel beer and eat free food. I buy the beer. Not eat the food yet."

The judge tipped his head back and laughed. "No. No. Let's leave the smell of beer and old tobacco, shall we. Once you're cleaned up, we'll go to Bescher's on Fifteenth Street. Best steak in Cheyenne. You need some red meat. I can tell."

"But. But. Why would you do that?"

"Son. John and Emily Laramie fed me many times when I studied in Boston, long before you were born, and that even though I was older than most students. You are John Laramie's son. I can do no less for you than they did for me."

"Laramie?"

"Yes, you are a Laramie."

"What is my white name?"

"I don't know, son. But maybe we can find out."

– 5 –

White Deer ate a man-sized steak, two baked potatoes, a side order of beans, four slices of sourdough bread with butter, and two slices of apple pie. His stomach felt stuffed to the base of his throat. "I can't swallow any more," he said.

"I reckon you'll sing a different song by the time we get home. Supper will be ready then, and you probably will be, too," Judge Hickey said. "Growing boys are like that. Shall we?"

"Shall we?"

"Yes. That means we should go."

"Yes. I have money."

"No. I will pay. You are my guest."

From Beschell's Restaurant, they walked east on Fifteenth Street to the livery. Gillicuddy came from the little office at the side of the barn as they approached.

"That job's waiting, you know," he said to White Deer. "Your bay is in the third stall, Judge."

"Thank you, Bowler. Do you have something the boy could ride?"

"Maybe he'd like to take a pick." Gillicuddy led them through the livery barn to a corral at the back. He waved at a bunch of horses on the far side. "You can ride any horse you want," he said.

White Deer went back into the barn and stopped at the second stall on the right. "This one?" he asked.

The stall held a small pinto of no more than fifteen hands. Its arched neck and small nose spoke of Arabian or maybe appaloosa ancestry.

Bowler Gillicuddy grinned. "No fooling you, eh, boy? That paint's as good a pony as you'll find between here and Texas. Sure. You can ride him. Just tell me you'll come to work here and he's yours as long as you're here."

White Deer said, "When should I come to work?"

Gillicuddy laughed out loud. "By God, boy, you'll do. Be here by sunup tomorrow. The pinto's yours to ride until you don't want to work here any more."

White Deer sheepishly got his chest from behind the old wagon and received permission to leave it against the tackroom wall. He retrieved the Colt revolver and its loads, and the rest of his money.

They turned north on Russell. "My place is about six miles out," Judge Hickey said. "Close enough to get to town easily, far enough for me to wind down on the way home so Martha doesn't have to deal with a cranky old man when I get there."

"Martha?"

"Oh, yes, Martha is my wife. Married nearly twenty years now. Happily, I might add."

White Deer considered this news. "Where are your children?" he asked.

Judge Hickey's face went sober. "Martha is unable to bear children," he said. "It was hard at first, but now we go to church and she teaches the children in Sunday school. That helps."

They came to a creek and rode along its western bank. "Crow Creek," the judge said, "but I've seen no more of those birds here than elsewhere."

"The Crows are tough warriors," White Deer said. "It is good to stay away from Crows."

"You know, your father was a policeman," Judge Hickey said suddenly. "He was a good one, too, an excellent officer. Emily operated a boarding house where I stayed. I knew them well. In fact, she was pregnant with you when I had to leave."

"Policeman?"

"Yes. A lawman. And a good one," the judge repeated.

White Deer felt warmth begin deep in his chest. His father was a lawman. Someone who caught those who did wrong and punished them. That was good.

"So John and Emily were lost at Fall Creek. Sad, that. They were moving on, rebuilding their lives. That fight was not a happy occurrence here in Dakota Territory. I hadn't thought about it, but our county carries the name of your parents, Laramie. Coincidental, I'm sure, but it is a fitting commendation." Judge Hickey seemed to be ruminating as much as carrying on a conversation with White Deer. "Arapahos raised you, you say."

"I was one of Lightning Cloud's village."

"What happened? What brings you to Cheyenne?"

"My mother died. My father took his village to Canada. He says the redcoats there allow Arapaho to live in their own way, not the white man's way." White Deer made no attempt to wipe away the tears that escaped his eyes. He held his head high.

"I'm going to get a scolding when we get home. Martha will say, 'Evan J. there you go bringing company home again without telling me.' How she expects me to tell her, I'll never know." Judge Hickey chuckled. "It's not like we have our own private telegraph."

"Evan Jay?"

"Yes. Evan J. That's my given name."

White Deer reined the pinto to a stop. "Judge," he called.

Judge Hickey stopped the bay and turned in his saddle. "What's wrong, son?"

"There was a big tough-looking man standing by me in the Bucket of Blood," White Deer said. "He talked with someone beside him. 'Got to teach old Evan Jay a lesson.' That's what he said.

"What did those men look like?"

White Deer told him, and Judge Hickey knew who they were. "Burt and Joc Everett," he said.

"Who?"

97

"Brothers. Our county was just created last year, and the governor appointed me judge here. One of the first things I did was send Ed Everett to jail."

"This Ed. He did something wrong?"

"He did. He rustled cattle from the Valentine outfit. A man does not steal cattle in this county. He was lucky not to be hanged."

"But why these brothers? Why get even?"

"Ed Everett died in prison. That and the two brothers were drunk and disorderly at the Little House in Cheyenne—that's a brothel. Rafe brought them in and I fined them each thirty-five dollars. They've got reason, in their own minds, at least."

"It was whiskey talk?"

"We can hope."

The night turned cold and White Deer wished Rafe had found his buffalo cape.

The judge reined up when they reached the rise that overlooked his property. "Too dark to see well," he said. "Light in the window. Still ..." He turned to White Deer. "Just in case, you wait here." Judge Hickey pulled a Colt Roots from a holster inside his coat, checked its loads, and put it back. "I'll ride down," he said. "If all is well, I'll fire a shot. Then you come in. If you don't hear a shot, ride for Cheyenne. Ride fast. Kill the horse if you have to, but ride hard and fast. Fetch Sheriff Adams and Rafe. Do you understand me?"

"May be those men wait for you."

"Maybe. But Martha's down there. I will ride in." The judge pulled his hat down tight. "Do what I say."

"Yes, sir."

Judge Hickey gigged the bay and sent it galloping down the hill toward his home. The one with a single light burning in its window.

The rising moon shed some light, but White Deer could not see well. He decided to disobey the judge's instructions. He walked the pinto to the bottom of the rise and took cover behind a copse of lodgepole pines.

Judge Hickey stood for a long moment after he dismounted the bay. White Deer was hidden in the copse before the judge got to the door. Just as he reached for the knob, the door opened and Joe Everett stepped out. He said something to the judge that made him take an involuntary step away. Joe backhanded Judge Hickey across the face.

No shot.

But White Deer was too close now. Besides, what would happen while he was riding those miles back to Cheyenne? Big Joe Everett didn't look like the type that sat around waiting for lawmen to show up.

As White Deer watched, Burt, the other Everett brother, came to join in the beating. They laughed as their fists punished the judge, a man who had done no wrong. But he made no move to protect himself. Strange. White Deer didn't see Judge Hickey as a man who placidly stood still as two big men slowly beat him to a pulp.

White Deer thought for a fleeting moment about going for the sheriff. *What would my father do? What would Lightning Cloud do?*

Both of his fathers offered the same answer. Those men were wrong. Those men must be stopped and punished. White Deer tethered the pinto to a pine sapling and started for the house.

He heard fists striking flesh. They sounded like village women pounding rawhide to make it soft and pliable. He used every shadow. He forgot the cold. He concentrated on the men beating Judge Hickey. Their attention was on the object of their rage.

A warrior does not hurry. Haste can only alert the enemy. Still, White Deer winced as hammer-like fists beat the man who had befriended him, the man who was a friend of his father. Judge Hickey now made little whimpers when the fists crashed into him. His legs could no longer support him, so Burt held him up while Joe punched.

"How's it feel, Judge?" Joe used a big foot, swinging it around and into Judge Hickey's belly. The judge could only groan. Blood-flecked spittle drooled from his battered lips. White Deer felt a white-hot coal of anger burn in his belly, but his anger did not affect his judgement. He used every wile he learned as an Arapaho warrior in training. He was in plain sight, but the two men beating Judge Hickey did not see him. He only moved when their attention focused on the target of their own anger. He reached the edge of the house and disappeared.

For some reason, the pinto neighed. Perhaps he wanted the company of the judge's bay mare.

"What's that?"

"A horse, stupid." *Splat.*

"Ain't in the corral."

Splat. "So have a look, asshole."

White Deer continued around the house, peering into each window he passed. At the very back, a window looked in on a bedroom. A candle flickered on the dresser. A woman sat tied to a chair with something that looked like a dishrag stuffed into her mouth. He pulled the old Colt Army from his waistband to use its butt to break the window. The woman saw him. She shook her head. Then lifted her chin. She lifted it again. White Deer pushed up on the window and the bottom half slid up. He climbed through. The woman looked frightened. He shushed her with a finger to his lips. She nodded.

He had no idea of the old Colt would fire, but he noticed a Henry rifle on pegs. He took it down carefully and jacked the lever. Empty. He catfooted to Martha and took the dishrag from her mouth. She gasped as if the rag had cut off her breathing.

White Deer put his mouth close to ear. "Bullets?"

"Top drawer," she whispered. She cleared her throat. "Please help Evan J. Please."

White Deer patted her on the shoulder and nodded. He turned to the dresser and opened the top drawer. A box of .44 rimfire nestled in the front corner. He grabbed it, dumped the cartridges out on the bed, and loaded the Henry.

Rifle loaded, White Deer snuck into the front room. He crouched by the door. Carefully, he eared back the hammer.

"Don't like this, Burt," a voice said. "Damn pinto horse tied in that bunch of pines, but they ain't no one around. Time to light a shuck, I'd say."

101

"Yeah. But these here assholes ain't dead yet. Only take a minute. Get the old lady. Let her watch our judgement on Ol' Evan Jay."

Burt Everett took a step toward the door as White Deer swung it open. "God damn," he shouted, clawing for his gun. Joe Everett drew first. As he raised his gun, White Deer triggered the Henry. Lightning Cloud's words echoed in his mind. *Look at what you want to hit. Let your heart guide your arrow.* Bullets had to be the same, and the bullet from the Henry smashed into Joe Everett's left shoulder, knocking him back and turning him away. He lost hold of his pistol, which dropped to the ground. Grunting with pain, Joe scrabbled for the fallen weapon.

Burt's Colt cleared leather and he fanned away three rounds, but White Deer was already moving. Three steps, and he dove headlong from the porch, holding the Henry out in front of him with both hands. He hit, rolled, and came up with the rifle ready. He jacked the lever and fired. A hole appeared like magic in Burt Everett's forehead. The big chunk of .44 caliber lead tumbled through his brain and exited the back of his head in a shower of gray matter, bone bits, and blood. The gunman collapsed like a rag doll.

Joe found his gun and snapped a shot at White Deer. The bullet tore into his thigh and his leg suddenly would not hold him up any more. He tipped and fell, keeping a firm hold on the rifle. He skittered away, Joe Everett's bullets chasing as he went. He gritted his teeth against the pain and stood. He faced Joe Everett dead on and began to sing his death song. He planted his feet and raised the Henry. Singing. Singing.

Joe fired and missed. White Deer sang. Joe thumbed the hammer back. White Deer sang. As Joe pulled the trigger, White Deer fired. Joe's bullet took White Deer in the muscle of his shoulder. White Deer's bullet plowed into and through the second button of Joe's shirt. He was dead before he hit the ground.

White Deer staggered to the porch and sat down on the top step. Sweat drenched him, though the night was cold. He bled.

Judge Hickey crawled over, his face an unrecognizable mass of lacerations, bruises, and dried blood, and his nose was swollen twice its usual size. He tried to say something, then tried again. All he could do was grunt.

At last his voice came. "You saved us, son," he said, his voice grating like chains over rock. "Hang on. I'll get Martha. Hang on. Hear me? Hang on. She'll patch you up. Hear?"

"Yes, sir," White Deer mumbled, then passed out.

* * *

Judge Hickey followed Martha into their extra room where White Deer slept. In the week since the exchange of shots with the Everetts, he'd stayed there. Martha stitched his wounds, a through-and-through in his left thigh and a wicked gouge in the muscle of his left shoulder. White Deer was up and around the second day, but Martha insisted on bringing breakfast into his room every morning. Today she had a stoneware bowl full of oatmeal, a pitcher of creamy milk, and a cut-glass bowl of brown sugar.

"Sure smells good, Mother Martha," White Deer said.

"If a man doesn't eat, he can't mend, son," she said as she placed the food on a small table by White Deer's bed.

"Thank you, Mother Martha, but don't you think it's about time I joined you and the judge for breakfast in the kitchen. I'd really like that."

Martha placed her hand on his brow. "Well. No fever. And you do walk about well. I suppose so. Tomorrow, then."

White Deer grinned.

"We're proud of you, son," the judge said. "You did a mighty brave thing the other night."

"The men did wrong," White Deer said. "Someone who does wrong must face what he does. If he changes his heart and does right things, then okay. But wrongs need to be set right. I just set the men right." White Deer concentrated on the porridge, coating the top with two heaping spoonfuls of brown sugar and pouring milk to the brim of the bowl.

"I wish we had sheriffs and marshals who thought like you," Judge Hickey said. "Your pa would be right proud of you, son. Your ma, too." A wistful look came over his face.

"Do you feel up to study?" Martha asked. She'd taken it upon herself to teach White Deer to read.

He swallowed a spoonful of oatmeal. "Yes. A man must be able to read. I know that now. But first I will eat." He spooned more porridge into his mouth. After he'd swallowed it he said, "Today I will ride Paint into Cheyenne. The man at the barn said he wanted me to work and I took his horse. I must keep my promise."

The judge nodded. "It's good to keep your promises, son." He paused a moment. "Look at me. Calling you 'son' as if you were a little boy. What was your name in Lightning Cloud's village?"

"My adult name is White Deer. My father Lightning Cloud said such a deer is very rare."

"White Deer." Judge Hickey rolled the name on his tongue. His face still wore scabs, and mottled black and green marks from the bruises gave him a wild look. His nose was now out of line, but it seemed to add character. "'Tis a good name. Keep it always. Still, I'd better write Boston for your birth name." He put a hand on White Deer's shoulder. "I'm sure you don't need this advice, but give Bowler Gillicuddy a full day's work."

White Deer finished the bowl of oatmeal. He looked at Martha, a question on his face.

"Oh! My! Yes, I forgot to bring the coffee." She bustled out of the room to the sound of her men's laughter.

* * *

White Deer now boarded at the livery. Just after he started work, Gillicuddy suggested he stay there, but Martha Hickey still drove up in her buggy every day but Sunday, bringing White Deer a lunch and an hour's worth of education. He looked forward to those lessons, and now read everything he could find, often going to sleep long after the sun went down.

"Hey, Cash." Gillicuddy called White Deer by that name ever since he'd overheard him insisting a customer pay "cash" for the livery's services. "Hey, Cash!"

"Be right there," White Deer hollered from the rear stall where he was rasping down a piebald sorrel's hooves. He put away the rasp and walked to the front of the livery, wiping his hands on his short canvas apron.

Judge Hickey stood with Gillicuddy just outside the barn door, where the sunshine warmed the day somewhat. The judge held a letter.

"Is that from the birth record place," White Deer asked.

"I'm afraid it's bad news, son. The building where the records were stored burned down. Nothing could be saved. I will keep looking, but for now, we just don't know what your parents named you. I'm sorry."

Bowler Gillicuddy squinted one eye and looked up at the sun. "Judge, around here we call him 'Cash.'"

"Cash?"

"Yep. He's strict with all the customers. Always gives them the best job he can do, but always insists on cash. Everyone wants Cash to care for their stock now. Talk about a man being an asset, that's Cash."

"If he's an asset, I'm sure you've adjusted his remuneration to reflect that value," the judge said with a stern voice.

"When he earns it," Gillicuddy said, "he's paid in cash."

"Cash Laramie." The judge looked at White Deer for a reaction and was met with a wide smile. "First big smile I've seen on your face for some time," he said.

"I have a name," White Deer said. "A man should have a name."

"That he should," the judge said. "Cash Laramie."

*   *   *

Cash buried the outlaw under enough rocks to keep the scavengers from gnawing on the flesh and bones, but he didn't waste time to make a cross. Crazy Ed wasn't Saint Peter bound.

His thoughts shot back to how quickly he had given up his White Deer name and sadness washed over him. He reached for the arrowhead around his neck. A long time had passed since he said his final goodbye to Elina and departed ways with Lightning Cloud. A tear welled in his eye as he touched the buffalo leather and ran his fingers down to the rough edges of obsidian, ending at the sharp point.

"I am sorry, Mother. I am sorry, Father. But know that I have not forgotten all that you did for me." His eyes traveled across the colorful dunes of El Desierto Pintado. "I'll never forget."

†

Other titles from BEAT to a PULP

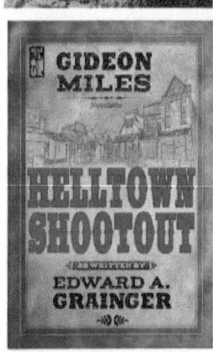
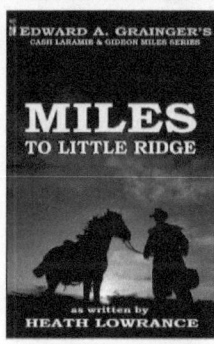
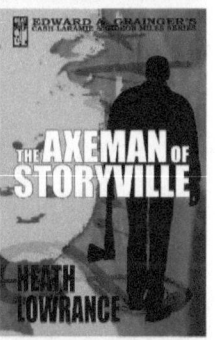